KU-657-531

LOST

'A marvellously written story'
Marie Claire

'This fictional child's-eye view of adult obsession,
etched with black humour and insight, see-saws
cleverly between despair and delight'
Harpers & Queen

'The hidden knowledge, the guilt and shame, runs
through Hans-Ulrich Treichel's short, excellent tale as
a flaw does through a tragic hero'
Daily Telegraph

'Finely translated by Carol Brown Janeway who
translated Bernhard Schlink's *The Reader* . . . faultlessly
written and intelligent'
The Times

'Brilliant . . . mesmerizing. The narrator's voice won't
let you go'
New York Times

'This is a subtle, sardonic, anguishing little book . . . as
an account of the unending effects of personal
trauma *Lost* is frightening'
Independent

'A funny and quietly devastating account of four
destroyed lives'
Metro London

Hans-Ulrich Treichel was born in 1952. He is a poet, essayist and professor of German literature at the University of Leipzig. He divides his time between Berlin and Leipzig. *Lost* has been translated into seventeen languages.

A note on the translator

Carol Brown Janeway's translations include Binjamin Wilkomirski's *Fragments*, Marie de Hennezel's *Intimate Death*, Bernhard Schlink's *The Reader* and Jan Philipp Remmetsma's *In the Cellar*.

Also by Hans-Ulrich Treichel

LIEBE NOT (1986)

SEIT TAGEN KEIN WUNDER (1990)

VON LEIB UND SEELE (1992)

DER EINZIGE GAST (1994)

HEIMATKUNDE ODER ALLES IST HEITER
UND EDEL (1996)

LOST

HANS-ULRICH TREICHEL

*Translated from the German
by Carol Brown Janeway*

PICADOR

First published 1999 by Pantheon Books, a division of Random House, Inc., New York
and simultaneously in Canada by Random House of Canada Limited, Toronto

Originally published in Germany as *Der Verlorene* by
Suhrkamp Verlag Frankfurt am Main in 1998

First published in Great Britain 2000 by Picador

This edition published 2001 by Picador
an imprint of Macmillan Publishers Ltd
25 Eccleston Place, London SW1W 9NF
Basingstoke and Oxford
Associated companies throughout the world
www.macmillan.com

ISBN 0 330 48037 5

Copyright © 1998 by Suhrkamp Verlag Frankfurt am Main
Translation copyright © 1999 Carol Brown Janeway

The right of Hans-Ulrich Treichel to be identified as the
author of this work has been asserted by him in accordance
with the Copyright, Designs and Patents Act 1988.

All rights reserved. No part of this publication may be
reproduced, stored in or introduced into a retrieval system, or
transmitted, in any form, or by any means (electronic, mechanical,
photocopying, recording or otherwise) without the prior written
permission of the publisher. Any person who does any unauthorized
act in relation to this publication may be liable to criminal
prosecution and civil claims for damages.

1 3 5 7 9 8 6 4 2

A CIP catalogue record for this book is available from
the British Library.

Typeset by SetSystems Ltd, Saffron Walden, Essex
Printed and bound in Great Britain by
Mackays of Chatham plc, Chatham, Kent

This book is sold subject to the condition that it shall not,
by way of trade or otherwise, be lent, re-sold, hired out,
or otherwise circulated without the publisher's prior consent
in any form of binding or cover other than that in which
it is published and without a similar condition including this
condition being imposed on the subsequent purchaser.

LOST

My brother squatted on a white blanket and laughed into the camera. That was during the war, my mother said, the last year of the war, at home. Home was the East, and my mother had been born in the East. As my mother spoke the words 'at home' she began to cry, as she so often did when the subject of my brother came up. His name was Arnold, like my father's. Arnold was a happy child, said my mother, looking at the photograph. She didn't say any more, and I didn't say anything either, and looked at Arnold squatting on a white blanket and being happy. I don't know what was making him happy, it was the war after all, and besides that he was in the East, and he was still happy. I envied him his happiness, I envied him the white blanket, and I envied him his place in the photo album, too. Arnold was right at the front of the album, ahead even of my parents' wedding pictures and the portraits of the grandparents, while I was way at the back. And

Arnold's picture was quite big, while most of the photos I was in were small, not to say tiny. Snapshots taken by my parents with what they called a Box Brownie, and apparently this box thing could only make little tiny photos. You had to look at the photos with me in them very carefully to recognize anything at all. For example, one of these tiny snapshots was of a pool with several children in it, and one of them was me. All you could see of me was my head, because I didn't know how to swim then, and I was sitting in the water, which came up almost to my chin. And my head was partly hidden by a child standing in the water in front of me, so that the minuscule photo with me in it only showed part of my head right above the surface of the water. And what's more there was a shadow on the visible part of my head, which was probably made by the child standing in front of me, so that the only bit of me you could really see was my right eye. While my brother Arnold looked not just happy but important even when he was a baby, in most of the photos from my childhood I am either only partly visible or sometimes not really visible at all. One of the times I was not really visible at all was in the photo of my christening. My mother held a white cushion on her arm, with a white coverlet over it. Under the coverlet was me, which you could tell because it had been pushed aside at the bottom of the cushion and the toes of a baby foot were peeking out. All subsequent photos taken of me in my childhood continued this tradition, one way or the other, except that in later photos the foot was replaced by a right arm, or half a profile, or an eye, as in the picture from the swimming pool. I would have accepted my truncated self in the family album, if my mother hadn't made a habit of reaching for the album to show me the pictures in it. Every time, the little tiny Box Brownie photos that showed me or rather various parts of me were leafed through hastily, while the photo of Arnold, which seemed life-size to me, was the object of endless contemplation. As a result I usually sat next to my mother on the sofa looking as miserable as I felt, and staring at cheerful and un-miserable Arnold, as my mother got more and more upset. I was still a small child when I became accustomed to my mother's tears, and I didn't spend any time wondering why Arnold's face made her cry so often. And the fact that although Arnold was my brother, I had never seen him in the flesh, didn't bother me in those first years, particularly because I was quite happy not having to share my room with him. At some point my mother explained what had happened to Arnold, inasmuch as she told me he had starved to death during their flight from the Russians. 'Starved,' said my mother, 'starved in my arms.' Because she herself had been more or less starving during the long trek from the East to the West, and she had no milk to feed the baby, and nothing else besides. When I asked if nobody else had had milk for the baby either, she said nothing, nor did she answer all my other, more detailed questions about the flight and my brother starving. So Arnold was dead, which was certainly very sad, but it made it easier for me to deal with his photo. Happy, easygoing Arnold even struck a chord in me, and I was proud to have a brother who was dead and still looked so happy and easygoing. I mourned Arnold and was proud of him, and I shared my room with him and wished him all the milk in the world. I had a dead brother and felt I had been singled out by fate. None of my playmates had a dead brother, let alone one who'd starved to death while fleeing the Russians.

Arnold had become my friend, and would have stayed my friend if my mother hadn't asked me one day for something she called a 'discussion'. She had never asked me to have a discussion before, and my father had never asked me to have one either. In my entire childhood and first teen-age years, I was never asked to have a discussion or anything resembling one. My father communicated with brief orders and instructions on how to do things, and my mother did talk to me now and then, but mostly it was talk about my brother Arnold and it ended in tears or silence. The discussion began with my mother saying that I was old enough now to know the truth. 'What kind of truth?' I asked her, because I was afraid it might be something to do with me. 'It's about your brother Arnold,' she said. In a way I was relieved that it had to do with Arnold again, but it upset me, too. 'What about Arnold?' I said, and my mother looked on the verge of tears once again, which made me ask spontaneously, but unreflectively, whether anything had happened to him. My mother settled that one with an irritated glance. 'Arnold,' she said without further preamble, 'Arnold isn't dead. He didn't starve either.' Now I was irritated too, and also a little disappointed. I should have kept quiet, but I asked my mother, again without thinking, what Arnold had died of instead. 'He didn't die,' she said again, her voice flat. 'He was lost.' Then she told me the story of how Arnold got lost, some of which I understood and some of which I didn't. The story was of a piece with Arnold dead of starvation, and at the same time it was a completely new one. Arnold had in fact endured starvation on the trek from East to West, and my mother had in fact had neither milk nor anything else for the child. But Arnold hadn't starved to death, he'd got lost and my mother was finding it difficult to give a clear picture of the reason why Arnold had disappeared. At some point – this much I understood – during the flight from the Russians, something dreadful happened. My mother didn't say what it was, she just kept saying that something dreadful happened during their flight from the Russians and that not even my father had been able to help her, nobody had been able to help her. Thousands of people had made the trek towards the West, and for a long time it had looked as if they would get through it more or less unharmed and keep putting a little more distance between themselves and the Russians. But one day, when they had just left a little farming village west of Königsberg, the Russians had suddenly appeared without warning out of the morning mist. They had neither seen nor heard anything all night long, no sound of engines, no sound of marching boots, no calls of '*Dawai! Dawai!*' Yet the Russians were suddenly there. Where there had been an empty field a moment ago, thirty or forty armed Russians were standing, and they broke into the moving column of fugitives to choose their victims exactly where my mother and father and Arnold were. They realized at once that something dreadful was going to happen, and as one of the Russians had already put his gun to my father's chest, my mother just had time to put her child in the arms of a passing woman, who luckily wasn't detained by any of the Russians. But the speed and panic of it all were such that she had no chance to exchange a single word with the woman, not even to call out little Arnold's name to her, and the woman disappeared immediately in the tide of refugees. The dreadful thing, said my mother, didn't exactly happen after all, since the Russians didn't shoot either her or my father. That had been the first thing they had feared, and that was why she had pushed little Arnold into the unknown woman's arms. But then, according to my mother, something dreadful did happen. 'But something dreadful happened after all,' she said. She started crying again when she said this, and I was sure that she was crying about Arnold, so to comfort her I told her that she'd really saved Arnold's life and she didn't have to cry, to which my mother said that Arnold's life had never been in danger. Neither had my father's, and neither had hers. Something dreadful had been done to her by the Russians, but they'd had no intention of taking her life or those of her family. They'd only been intent on one thing. But she'd been too quick in fearing for her life and the life of her child, and if she were honest, she'd been too quick to give the child away. She hadn't even been able to call out Arnold's name to the woman in the panic and confusion, and all the woman had been able to do was clutch the child to her and keep running. 'Arnold's alive,' said my mother, 'but he has another name.' 'Maybe he was lucky,' I said, 'and they named him Arnold again,' at which my mother looked at me with such incomprehension and sadness that the blood rushed to my head and I was ashamed. But I'd only said it because I was angry at Arnold. Because I was only just beginning to understand that Arnold, my un-dead brother, had the leading role in the family and had assigned me a supporting part. I also under-stood that Arnold was responsible from the very beginning for my growing up in an atmosphere poisoned with guilt and shame. From the day of my birth, guilt and shame had ruled the family, without my knowing why. All I knew was that whatever I did, I felt guilty and ashamed as I did it. For example, I always felt guilty and ashamed at meals, regardless of the food that was set in front of me. If I ate a piece of meat, I had a bad conscience, and it was just as bad if I ate a potato or dessert. I felt guilty to be eating, and ashamed to be eating. I absolutely knew that I felt guilty and ashamed, but I could not explain to myself why the innocent child that I was should be shamed by a piece of meat or a potato or should feel guilty. I was just as baffled about why I had to feel guilty when I listened to the radio, rode my bicycle, or went for a walk or an outing with my parents. Yet the walks or outings with my parents, which always took place on Sundays, weighed on my conscience and triggered a great sense of shame. When I walked along the main street of our town with my mother and father, I felt ashamed that I was walking along the main street of our town with them. When we drove out of town in the black limousine, which my father had bought himself when the business was going well, to head for the Teutoburg Forest which lay nearby, I felt ashamed and guilty that we were heading for the Teutoburg Forest. When we'd finally got there and were walking along the same old path to the so-called Bismarck Tower, I felt ashamed and guilty that we always chose the same old path. And of course once we did finally get there and climbed the Bismarck Tower to take in the view of the plain and the distant spire of the church in my home town, I felt ashamed and guilty all over again. The walks and outings I went

on with my parents were regular penitential pro-
cessions of shame and guilt. My parents also
seemed depressed and tormented and I always
had the sense that they dragged themselves out of
the house every Sunday as if on orders. And yet
they would never have considered giving up the
Sunday outings, since the Sunday outings served
first to replenish strength for the working week
and second were required by Christian respect for
the Sabbath. All the same, my parents were
incapable of enjoying freedom or relaxation even
in sudden bursts. At first I put this inability down
to the combination of their Swabian-pietistic and
East Prussian origins. For I knew from stories told
me by my parents that neither the pietistic Swa-
bian nor the East Prussian is in any way equipped
to actually enjoy either freedom or relaxation. But
then I realized that their incapacity for freedom
and relaxation was all tied up with my lost brother
Arnold and the dreadful thing that the Russians
had done to them, my mother in particular. And
I imagined that the spoiled outings made me
more miserable than my parents, since they were
convinced that man was not put on earth to go
on outings but to work, which meant that the

outings were more or less spoiled to begin with. I, on the other hand, loved outings and would have been happiest if there was an outing every day. Admittedly not the ones that I went on with my parents. I developed such antipathy for those that my parents could only make me go along under threat of punishment. The most wonderful punishment they held over me was house arrest. But I only attained the bliss of Sunday house arrest after I'd managed to develop a special form of travel sickness, which proved effective even on shorter outings. Its chief symptom was a physical inability to tolerate movement, but it made a certain distinction between me moving my own body and things moving me. When I moved my own body, during our neighbourhood walks, for example, I usually got dizzy and had to sit on a bench. If I was the one being moved, I had to throw up. Mostly I had to throw up when we were on outings in the new black limousine, whereas when we were driving in the silver grey Ford, the Humpback Taunus as it was called, I never had to throw up. The old Ford was the only vehicle in my childhood that didn't make me feel sick. But of course my father sold it again as soon as his business began to do well, first to buy an Opel Olympia and then the black limousine with the shark's teeth. In the Opel Olympia I had thrown up not regularly, just frequently. Whereas I threw up regularly in the black limousine, which meant not only that I was often driven back home, pale and exhausted, with my clothes all dirty, but the car had to be thoroughly cleaned and aired out after each failed outing before it could be occupied again. Eventually my parents decided to stop using the car for Sunday outings but to take the train that ran between our town and the Teutoburg Forest, and hence was known as the Teutoburg Forest Train. I still had to throw up in the Teutoburg Forest Train, but the carriages were filled with wooden seats, and besides I could retreat to the toilet if there was time. My parents would have had no problem coming to terms with me throwing up regularly on the Teutoburg Forest Train, if it hadn't been for the other passengers, who took the brunt of my vomiting if I couldn't get to the toilet and threw up on the floor or the benches. Eventually my parents gave in, and I was allowed to spend Sundays alone at home, and those are some of the happiest memories of my whole childhood. Actually it was the first fifteen minutes after my parents left when I felt completely happy and free. After the fifteen minutes were over, a feeling of anxiety and loneliness set in, which I tried to escape by all sorts of diversionary tactics. One was to sit at the open window in the living room with my eyes closed and try to recognize the makes of the passing cars by the sound of their engines. In time I became so good at this game that I guessed most of the cars before they'd even reached our house. It has to be said, however, that the majority of cars back then were variants on the base models of Volkswagen or DKW. It was harder with foreign cars, but only very rarely did I fail to identify the strange engine noise, open my eyes and follow a car that I'd never seen before. My win ratio in this game reached about 90 per cent, closely followed by my boredom, so I switched to a self-imposed requirement of fifty cars per Sunday, after which I would have to find some other form of relaxation. This other relaxation consisted of staying glued to the radio, which resulted in my sitting hour after hour in front of the illuminated display, constantly changing stations. Listening to the radio bored me; staying glued to the radio bored me even more. In some way I already knew as a child, long before the arrival of television, that the radio was no television. The radio didn't satisfy me, it only distracted me from the sense of oppressive anxiety in the house until suddenly, in mid station change, I stumbled on someone talking in Russian – or what sounded like Russian. Naturally I was astonished that there was a Russian station on East Westphalian Radio, but I also knew from my parents' stories that the Russians were capable of anything. Although I didn't understand a word of what the Russian on the radio was saying, I listened greedily to the strange sounds. And the longer I listened to the Russian's words, which sometimes sounded like orders or instructions and then slipped into a kind of melancholy singsong again, the more it seemed that not only could I understand individual snippets of the speech, I also imagined that what the Russian was saying had something to do with me and my family. Naturally I wasn't sure, but as I sat in my Sunday solitude by the radio, I was pursued by the recurrent thought that the Russian was talking about the infamous and dreadful thing that had been done to my parents, and especially my mother, and that the airwaves were now full of this infamy and dreadfulness. Luckily my father's financial success allowed him to acquire a television, so that I could extricate myself from the disturbing force of the radio and particularly the Russian station. And it was my father, who had no objections to my spending my Sundays alone for hours in front of the radio, who found it unendurable that I should spend those same hours in front of the television. Yes, he had bought a television, but he couldn't stand it being switched on. And if it was switched on, then it could only be switched on with his permission, which could be revoked at any moment. The television could only be switched on when my father gave his permission, but when he did give his permission, he did it so unwillingly, sometimes even angrily, that the pleasure of watching television was immediately spoiled. Besides which, from one second to the next my father could decide that the television must be switched off because he had something to say. It was absolutely impossible for him to say anything to me while the television was on. And naturally my father, who normally said

very little to me and could look straight past me
for hours without ever addressing a word to me,
always had something to say to me while the
television was on. In the process of which he not
only couldn't stand to have the television on, he
also could not possibly turn off the television
himself. Instead, he said, 'Television off,' or just
'Box off,' and I immediately leapt from my chair
and switched the machine off. The conversation
that then followed was nothing but instructions
about new things I had to do. Either it occurred
to him that the yard needed to be swept, or it was
a question of carrying a cardboard box of dis-
carded clothing or household things up to the
attic; or a letter needed to be posted or a form
delivered to the local authorities. I often thought
my father did nothing while the television was on
but think up tasks that still needed to be done. As
soon as he sat down in front of the television, his
mind went into gear and pondered what might
still need to be done, so that it was never possible
for me to watch a broadcast all the way to the
end, even in bits, in his company. The only time
my father liked television was in the company of
his older sister Hilde, who had been a widow since

the war and visited us regularly. If my father
judged television's usefulness by the formula 'If
you're watching, you're not working,' my aunt
considered it an invention of the Devil, which put
man in the position of being able to conquer time
and space and simultaneously robbed him of his
own four walls and abandoned every corner of
privacy to the world and its impulses. Aunt Hilde
was one of the greatest media teetotallers I've ever
known. The only periodical she was interested in
was a weekly called *Our Church*. The magazine was
brought right into our kitchen-living room every
Thursday by volunteers from the congregation
with the cry 'Church notes' and laid on the table.
Even the local newspaper aroused her suspicions,
and what interested her most in the church notes
was the list of old people's birthdays and the
weekly Bible selection. The weekly reading in
particular commanded my aunt's special attention. While she simply absorbed the details of the
old people's birthdays, she studied the current
weekly reading all over again every day and did
exactly what the editors of the church notes
hoped would be the result of their paper: she
made the church notes weekly lesson her own,

and for as long as the week lasted, she would read and ponder it. Aunt Hilde had her own estab-lished place at the kitchen table, as did the church notes. If a visitor saw the church notes lying open on the kitchen table, he knew that my aunt was visiting. My aunt also used to spend her evenings reading the church notes and pondering the weekly lesson, which wasn't a problem until the day the television got bought. It didn't just disturb her reading, it was also an invention of the Devil. But it also made her curious, which delighted my father, whom nothing amused as much as the temptations to which his pious sister felt herself subjected. My aunt solved the conflict insofar as she sat with her back to the television when it was on. She didn't look at it, but she listened. And as she listened, she also watched my father, my mother, and me watching the television. While my parents weren't bothered by being watched by my aunt watching television, I always felt she was not just watching me but seeing right through me. My aunt watched me and I was ashamed that she was watching me. When she turned her back to the television, she made it into a radio, which was apparently more acceptable to her religious sensibilities. Radio was allowed; television was a sin. She followed the voices, but she didn't want to fall under the power of the images. My aunt shielded herself from the images, and the images worked their way into the unprotected remainder of the family, i.e., mostly my mother and me. My father was immune to the images in that the only thing working in his brain was an extensive, image-proof program for organizing and assigning tasks as they fell due. My mother and I, on the other hand, ended up in front of the TV set as often as we could, and preferably when my father wasn't in the house. In any case we only enjoyed these hours in front of the TV so long as no intimacies occurred on the screen. The moment an intimate scene came on, we both froze in front of the TV and the room was filled with such embarrassment and shame that we hardly dared to breathe. Even the most harmless scene with a kiss in it made me long for the film to move on and the threatening scene to dissolve. But deliverance often didn't come then either, and the sense of shame lingered after the intimate scenes had vanished from the screen. It was enough that the two of us were together in front of the TV for the blood to rush to our faces. We sat glowing hotly in the darkened room and didn't dare move. When we sat in front of the TV we felt ashamed, even though I have no idea of what. Perhaps it had nothing to do with the intimacy on the TV, and what we were ashamed of was our intimacy in front of the TV. Perhaps it also had to do with my brother Arnold. When the atmosphere became too oppressive, my mother switched the TV off. Without uttering a word, she would leap to her feet, press the button, and leave the room. I didn't object, I was pleased she'd turned it off and I didn't have to feel the blood pulsing in my head any more. The silent TV made me feel better, but even better was my mother's leaving the room and finding something to do elsewhere in the house. The more she found to do in the house, the less she could be overcome by shame and guilt. And to tell you the truth, almost all my mother did was find things to do in the house. Just as my father did nothing but busy himself with business. My father, who began by running a lending library, then moved on to a food store and finally a meat and sausage whole-sale operation, clearly found his relaxation in

---

work. The lending library flourished for only a few years. TV and cheap paperback novels put an end to it. The grocery store flourished for a bit longer, but it didn't satisfy my father. He didn't want to sell sausage by the gram, he wanted to sell it by the kilo and the hundredweight. As a food store owner he himself was a customer of a meat and sausage wholesaler. When he found out that other food store owners were also unhappy with the wholesaler, he decided to become a wholesaler himself. He got all the relevant data from the local office of trade and industry, went to evening classes for a time, then took the qualifying exam to trade as a wholesaler. The food store was leased out, the food store owner's apron hung up on its nail and replaced with a two-piece suit. My father used his contacts with the other food store owners in the region who were his former colleagues and now became his customers. They trusted him, because he had been one of them, and he didn't let them down. It wasn't enough to supply high-quality products, according to my father, you also had to know how to listen to people's concerns. When he made the rounds of his customers, it was first and foremost to talk about their concerns. The order books seemed to fill up almost by themselves after that. The food store owners had a lot of concerns. A food store owner's life was one long concern. Or so it seemed to me back then, when I went with my father on his tour of customers and was able to listen in on his conversations with the owners. One of the chief concerns was spoilage of supplies. People who bought from the food stores wanted fresh produce. But what was first and foremost fresh produce to the customer was first and foremost perishable produce to the shop owner. If the customers stayed away, the food spoiled. If less produce was laid in, there was the risk of not being able to supply the customers' wants. So more supplies were laid in again and along with the supplies came the worry about the spoilage of the supplies. The food store owners were working constantly against time. The clock ticked on, and with every passing minute the lettuce wilted, the bananas browned, the sausage discoloured, and the mould ran riot. If customers didn't come, the food store owner stood there in the middle of his perishable produce and watched it perishing. Most store owners my father visited were both frantic and depressed. Many of them had stomach problems, which meant that they could only indulge sparingly in their own offerings. With others, it was the heart, with some, the nerves. I cannot remember a single store owner I ever met who didn't have health problems. Another problem was the competition. 'Competition is the life of business,' my father used to say once he was back outside one food store and on his way round the corner to visit the next. But when he was in the store listening to its owner complaining about the other owners, he didn't say, 'Competition is the life of business'; at most he said, 'Life is a struggle,' or some such thing. Yet another problem for the owners was the customers. 'No customer, no turnover,' was my father's comment when they complained. But sometimes the owners retorted that a customer was no guarantee of a sale. Because customers, especially customers in food stores, were nothing if not choosy, likely to be quite sensitive, often tight with their money and, as if all that weren't enough, incapable of making up their minds. He could take it, one of the owners said, if a customer insisted that what he wanted was one hundred grams of cervelat and he expected it to be one hundred grams exactly. But it made him ill when the customers just stood there in front of the counter, unable to make up their minds. There were customers, said one owner, who deliberately tried to make him ill by not making up their minds. Just when he thought they'd decided for the beer sausage, for example, as opposed to the blood sausage, they would recant and say no to the beer sausage without getting anywhere near saying yes to the blood sausage or anything else for that matter. They pestered him relentlessly while other customers had to wait just to be served. It had even happened to him, said one owner, that one customer had complained so loudly about another hopelessly indecisive customer that the former had left the shop in a huff while the latter still kept standing paralyzed in front of the sausage counter, bringing the entire operation to a halt. But worst of all were the ones who first couldn't make up their minds and then spelled out their wishes in ten-gram units, fifty grams of beer sausage on the one hand and fifty of cervelat on the other, although he should know that it could also be less, forty grams, for example, but didn't have to be, which drove him absolutely nuts. He sometimes saw himself as a druggist, having to measure out such hyper-fine quantities of sausage or cheese on the scales. The owners' melancholia made such a deep impression on me that without ever being aware of it, I transferred this sadness onto the goods themselves and viewed particular foods as something depressing until I was quite grown up. I was particularly moved by produce that was fresh and therefore perishable; years later I was still amazed by how downcast I could become in front of shelves of vegetables or a display of fresh sausages. A display of fresh sausages, on the other hand, could bring my father to euphoria. Particularly if they'd been supplied by him. But it was also because he came from farming stock that meat and sausage were not just the remains of a slaughtered animal, but something absolutely alive. In contrast to the owners who dealt in all kinds of foodstuffs, it was the so-called fresh meats that raised his spirits. One of his favourite dishes was a fresh cutlet. A fresh cutlet to him was as fresh as fresh air or fresh water. Better even than a fresh cutlet to my father was a fresh pig's head, which of course appeared on the table only twice a year, once in spring and once in fall; my father collected it himself from one of the farmers who supplied him, and brought it home. When my father arrived with the fresh pig's head (fresh meaning just severed from the pig), still bloody and all wrapped up in greaseproof paper, all members of the family had to gather in the kitchen to look at it. As far as I was concerned, one pig's head was like any other, but to my father each pig's head was unique, and sometimes after he'd set the pig's head down on the table, he even said, 'This time it's a particularly fine pig's head,' with great satisfaction. When I asked my father what distinguished a particularly fine pig's head from a less fine one, he said that a particularly fine pig's head was symmetrical, whereas a lesser pig's head was asymmetrical. By extension, according to my father, you could extrapolate from a pig's head to the pig in its entirety, and a fine head was connected inevitably to the body of a fine, that is to say muscular, pig with an even distribution of fat. The pig's head came with pig's blood. Pig's blood was almost as important to my father as the pig's head. 'Pig's blood is the sap of life,' my father said, and if it had been up to him I would have been raised on pig's blood, not milk. The blood was transported in tin cans and had to make the journey from the farm to my parents' house at top speed. If my father was held up it fell to me to fetch the blood from the farmer's. Transporting the blood would not normally have bothered me, particularly since I loved visiting the farmhouses because you always went past all the animals before you got to the living quarters. Where it became hard was that the blood to be carried home was poured into the cans directly from the pig. I had seen often enough how milk got from the cow into the can, but I had never imagined how blood got from a pig into the can. The blood got from the one to the other in such a horrible way that I watched it once and on subsequent blood transport duty I stayed in the farmer's kitchen until the can was full. The one glimpse I had of the animal, stabbed, twitching, squealing wildly, with a fountain of blood jetting from its carotid artery, upset me so much that I only took part in the ritual feasts of the pig's head reluctantly after that, and would have avoided them altogether if my father had allowed it. I would also have found the feasts of the pig's head easier if they had involved only one meal each time. But in some miraculous fashion my mother knew how to get so many meals out of one pig's head that we could live off it for ages. It proved itself a veritable horn of plenty, which released an incredible variety of dishes: pig's cheek and pig's tongue, pig's ear and pig's muzzle, pig's head broth and pig's head spread. It could all be smoked or grilled, boiled or roasted, dried or preserved, and was further enhanced by the use of pig's blood, which you could add to soup and make sausage with, and could even be baked or boiled down and put into preserving jars. Truth to tell the spring pig's head lasted almost all the way to fall, and the fall pig's head lasted into the New Year, so that we lived off pig's head and pig's blood products virtually all year round. But the feast of feasts was the pig's brain, which came to the table the same day my father brought the head and I brought the blood home. This was in some sense our version of the farmer's slaughter-day celebration; guests were invited, and this also made it a significant occasion for my father because it reminded him of slaughter days on his parents' farm. My father should have inherited the farm and become a farmer himself, and at least on the day when he and his family and his guests gathered to eat the pig's brain, he felt himself to be one. 'Brains make you smart,' he said, which made it quite impossible for me even to hope that I might be delivered from having to eat the pig's brains, for in my father's eyes, if I was lacking in something it was an adequate supply of brains. He could sometimes be generous and let me off having to eat blood soup or blood pudding, but when it came to brain, he was deaf to all compromise. I must also admit that although the sight of the brains made me feel ill, I actually liked taking part in the evening feast when they were served, because it was the only time things in my parents' house were so gay and relaxed. In some way, the dinner of pig's brain intoxicated my father and his guests with merriment. Particularly when the guests were friends of my father who came from the East as he did and should have become farmers too, dinner could be accompanied by never-ending laughter, and I would try to get the soft mess of brains down my throat unchewed as quickly as possible and would have no idea what they were laughing about, because pig's brain dinner produced conversation about virtually nothing except eating, and when it wasn't about eating, it was about killing animals. Most of my father's acquaintances slaughtered animals themselves or had once done so, so every one of them had tales to tell about slaughtering. Naturally it wasn't all about slaughtering pigs, but mostly about slaughtering smaller animals, hens, rabbits, ducks, geese and doves, because these could be slaughtered on their own even if you no longer owned a farm and lived in a rented apartment. The laughter that was unleashed by the tales of slaughtering was neither mean-spirited nor bloodthirsty, more peaceable. There was hearty, eye-twinkling mirth when, for example, somebody told the story of the headless chicken spouting blood that leapt into the lap of his grandmother who was dozing in a garden chair. Whereas I occasionally had nightmares after these dinner conversations and spent the night helplessly chopping heads off chickens, wringing pigeons' necks, cracking rabbits' skulls, and sticking knives into pigs' necks, the pig's brain dinner acted as a tranquilizer on my father, so that this man who

HANS-ULRICH TREICHEL

was otherwise so choleric and prone to rages had
such a forgiving look in his eyes that I thought I
would never have to be afraid of him again. My
mother, on the other hand, was quiet and withdrawn as always during the pig's brain dinners.
She did seem to be happy that my father and
their guests were so relaxed, but even I could feel
the strain she was under as the hours of rare high
spirits passed. And the feast evenings almost
always ended the same way: at a certain point my
father and the guests began to speak softly and
eventually stopped speaking altogether. They sat
beside each other mute and didn't say a word. My
mother would also spend the next few days being
uncommunicative and almost mute herself, as if
she were doing penance for the good dinner and
the laughter with a vow of silence. My father did
his penance in work. The more my mother
seemed liable to be paralyzed by the burden of
memories, the busier my father became. Having
been through the experience of losing house and
home twice, after each of the two world wars, and
having arrived empty-handed in East Westphalia
after the second, he had now built himself an
'existence' for the third time. He could have lived

in peace, but there was no peace. He rebuilt the house. The moment the food store had been transformed into a meat wholesale business, he set to work remodelling. He did it so fundamentally that the new house was nothing like the old house at all. The timber-framed building that had once been the coach and mail stop for the town was gutted, its walls removed right up to the rafters. The straw and clay filler was taken out, and some of the rafters too. The house got steel girders and smooth plaster. The windows were changed from casements to ones that tilted, and they never got frost flowers on them any more, the way they used to in years past, because they were double-glazed. The wooden front door with its iron handle became a glass door with a brass surround. The house had once been my childhood labyrinth, with long corridors, deep built-in cupboards, and unexpected stair landings, behind which more corridors stretched away, leading to other connecting doors and landings. It gave me pleasure to roam through the house, just as it gave me pleasure to go and see the attic crisscrossed with rafters and wooden braces – my magic forest, but also my place of terror. The attic must once have served as a storeroom and warehouse, because there was a trapdoor set into the floor, with a wooden winch fixed above it to haul up heavy loads. When I opened the trapdoor, I could see into a room I'd never been into, and which appeared to have no other entrance. I would have had to let myself down on the rope to get into it. It was way below me, lower than the floor below the attic. Maybe lower even than the ground floor. It was in semi-darkness, and I couldn't make out how large it was. I would have given anything to know if there was a door to the room, but I didn't dare ask my parents. I didn't even dare tell them that I'd opened the trapdoor and looked down. The attic got rebuilt too and turned into living space. The rebuilding took away my childhood labyrinth, straightened it out, gutted it, let the light in. The corners, nooks, long passageways had disappeared along with the built-in cupboards, connecting doors, and unexpected stair landings. Naturally the trapdoor went too, and with it the only entry to the hidden room. Yet curiously the area under the trapdoor was the same size after the reconstruction that it had been before. Not one square metre had been gained, and I was convinced that the room still existed, even if it was unfindable and impenetrable. After the rebuilding was finished, my mother had a breakdown. The doctor diagnosed strain and ordered her to go on a cure. The treatment lasted several weeks, and on weekends my father went to visit my mother in the clinic, while I was allowed to stay and guard the house. After one of these visits my father told me that my mother was doing better, but she was far from well. One reason for her illness was certainly all the exertion involved in the rebuilding. The real reason, however, was that she had never got over the loss of my brother Arnold. At the same time, according to my father, she felt that I, on the other hand, had got over the loss of my brother very well. I had got over it so well, in fact, that for years my mother hadn't trusted herself to tell me the truth about Arnold. At which point I told my father that my mother had told me the truth long ago. 'Arnold', I said, 'didn't starve to death, Arnold was lost.' When my father didn't react, I repeated, 'Arnold didn't starve to death, Arnold was lost.' My father still didn't react and seemed to be turning thoughts over in his mind. Perhaps I should have told him

that I hadn't felt any loss at all. When you came
right down to it, I hadn't lost anyone anyway. I
had only learned that my parents had lost and yet
not lost someone. And when I had discovered that
Arnold hadn't starved, but had just been lost, the
only loss I could be said to have suffered was that
I'd lost a dead brother, who'd died, what's more,
while fleeing the Russians. Now I didn't have a
dead brother, I had a lost one. That was hardly a
plus for me. But how could I explain this to my
father? And before I could think about it any
further, my father said, 'We're looking for him.'
'Who?' I said. 'Arnold,' said my father, without
noticing how mad my question was. 'Have been
for years.' I didn't say anything to that, so my
father explained that he and my mother had
already spent years searching for Arnold with the
help of the missing persons service of the Red
Cross, but that they hadn't wanted to burden me
with this knowledge. And now, after all these
years, they really had found someone who might
be Arnold. 'You've found him?' I asked, and even
as I uttered the question, I sensed the old sick
feeling return. 'Perhaps,' said my father. 'It's not
certain. For us to be absolutely sure, we're going

to need your help.' I had never heard my father speak like this to me before. He was talking to me as if I were a friend. Or at the very least a customer. He wanted to ask me for something. My father had never asked me for anything. He had only always said what had to be done, and then I did whatever that was. He hadn't ever had such a long conversation with me either. The tone in my father's voice made me uneasy, I felt faint, and I wished I could have given way to my old habit and thrown up. It would be necessary, my father said, to undergo various tests to establish our relationship to the boy in question. And I would have to submit to these tests as well. 'How did you find him?' was what I wanted to know, and I imagined us soon not being three but four together at the lunch table and I wouldn't just have to share dessert, I'd have to share my room as well, or even move out of it altogether to make space for my big brother. For the Arnold I knew from the photograph was an infant, but he'd been born before the end of the war, and was therefore several threatening years older than I was. 'We told the missing persons service when and where Arnold was lost,' said my father, 'and that there's a noticeable cowlick in his hair on the right side of his head. Subsequently we received word from the Red Cross that one of the foundlings entrusted to them has a noticeable cowlick in the right side of his hair.' This piece of news, according to him, had raised hopes in both him and my mother that Arnold had been found. Already at this point my mother was more or less sure that the child in the foundling home, who didn't even have a name, but was identified by the Red Cross simply as foundling 2307, was her child. Naturally they wanted to see the child with the pronounced cowlick on the right side of his head at once, but the authorities wouldn't permit it. To put it in a nutshell, many children had got lost as they fled, and arrived in the West without parents. And one of the official experts had told them that again and again most parents would identify as theirs any child who could be considered a possibility on the basis of the first flickers of evidence. Some parents, according to the expert, only needed to be told that the child in question was blond or brunette, and they would identify it as theirs. And there would always be some despairing set of parents who wanted to see a child who would turn out finally not to be theirs, which meant that they'd already had to confront some of the foundling children with a stream of possible new parents, which led to terrible disappointments, particularly for the children. But in our case, my father said, the pronounced cowlick on the right had only been the beginning. During an appointment at the relevant search bureau they had showed him photos of so-called foundling 2307, and both he and my mother had immediately recognized their son Arnold in the child, even if the child in the photos was almost a young man. But in such matters, said my father, it was instinct that talked, not intellect. Besides, foundling 2307 not only had a pronounced cowlick on the right, he had, according to information in possession of the search service, been in the same trek that my father and mother had been in as they fled the East. Moreover it had not only been the same trek, it had been the same day, 20 January 1945, when the boy was laid in an unknown woman's arms. And this without the woman's finding out the boy's name. The woman hadn't even been able to get a good look at the face of the person who laid the child in her arms, for the latter had been almost entirely veiled in a shawl. This was not so much against the cold, as that all young women had wrapped themselves in shawls back then so as not to be recognizable as young women. My mother wrapped herself in a shawl too. The first people the Russians threw themselves on, said my father, were young women. Which meant that they saw through the shawl trick quite quickly and consequently chose women with covered faces to throw themselves on. These could also turn out to be old women. According to my father, in principle no woman was safe from the Russians, be she young or old. And what this told me was that my mother must not have been safe from the Russians either. Most likely the Russians had thrown themselves on my mother too, but I wasn't really clear what exactly it meant when the Russians threw themselves on someone. My father said that the boy had not only been on the same trek and handed over to an unknown woman on the same day that my mother handed Arnold over to an unknown woman. The boy didn't just have a certain resemblance to the photo in the album, he also resembled my father and to some extent my mother. Admittedly the resemblance to him and my mother was not so great that you could conclude a family relationship without any other evidence. But the boy had an absolutely astonishing resemblance to me, his putative brother. This resemblance was so strong that my mother and he himself were utterly convinced on that fact alone that the boy must be Arnold. The authorities, on the other hand, said my father, were far less convinced that the boy must be Arnold, even if the expert on the case could agree on the basis of photos that the boy in the foundling home looked astonishingly like me, his putative brother. 'The boy', said my father, 'looks as if he were carved out of your face.' An idea which made me so physically queasy that although I didn't have to throw up, I got some kind of stomach cramp that reached up to my face, shot through my cheeks, and ended behind my forehead. It was almost as if I were feeling the cuts as Arnold was being carved out of my face, and the cuts were turning into a rain of blows and stabs of pain that ran through my face and caused me to grimace. What's there to grin about, said my father, who had no idea of the pain I was feeling and saw only the rude boy in me. The companionable conversation between friends or with a customer metamorphosed into the usual father–son conversation, in which he told me that after my mother had finished her cure and things had been organized at home, we would be visiting an institute to undergo the necessary tests that would confirm our relationship with Arnold. The stomach cramp had relaxed meanwhile, but I still suffered from facial twitches, especially when I was under stress, which not only brought on an involúntary grin, but also brought tears to my eyes. It was this last that made my father send me to the doctor. He diagnosed a trigeminal neuralgia which was more or less untreatable, as its causes were unknown. In the worst cases they would paralyze the trigeminal nerve, but that could entail a disruption of the entire facial musculature, which was why it was not recommended. In the doctor's opinion, the best thing to do in my case would be to wait. Maybe one day they'd discover the cause of my affliction, and perhaps the affliction would go away of itself. It would not be the first time that a trigeminal neuralgia disappeared as suddenly as it had appeared. The trigeminal neuralgia didn't disappear, it con-

tinued to plague me at lengthening but nonetheless regular intervals with attacks that were like
a surge of electrical current. I had no need to
search for causes, I was sure that my facial twitches
were connected with Arnold, and in particular
with what my father called an amazing likeness. I
didn't want to look like anyone, particularly not
my brother Arnold. The supposedly amazing likeness made me feel less and less like myself. Every
look in the mirror grated on my nerves. I didn't
see me, I saw Arnold, and he was getting less
appealing all the time. If only he had starved to
death during the escape. Instead he was interfer-
ing in my life. And in my appearance. I longed
for a Third World War so that he would starve to
death after all. But the Third World War never
came. Instead my mother came back from
her cure, and was as sad as before. Her mood
lightened a little when my father said that a plain-
clothes policeman would be coming to visit that
afternoon. The plain-clothes policeman came
accompanied by our local policeman, Mr
Rudolph, who was a sort of friend of the family,
and gave my parents help with anything to do
with the police, for which my father rewarded him

with regular parcels of meat and sausage. The plain-clothesman had come to take our finger-prints, so that they could be compared with Arnold's. He pressed our fingers one after the other onto an ink-pad, and then pressed our blackened fingertips onto a special index card. The man operated with practised efficiency, and the whole procedure was over disappointingly fast. I had expected more from the visit of a plain-clothesman. The only noteworthy thing was that I was allowed to get my fingers dirty in the presence of my parents, and that my parents got their fingers dirty too. But my parents wouldn't allow me to have my wish of keeping my fingers black and going to school that way. Even before the plain-clothesman was all the way out of the house, my mother was scrubbing the ink off my fingers with a nail brush. The next test was a blood analysis. Just as our fingers were to be compared with Arnold's, so was our blood. About six weeks after our family doctor took the blood samples and sent them off, my parents got the results. The letter came from the Institute of Forensic Medi-cine at the University of Münster and contained the results of both the fingerprint and the blood comparisons. The information about the finger-prints, which were no longer called fingerprints but bacciform finger patterns, was all couched in words such as 'diverse central pockets', 'double loops', 'ridges' and 'whirls', all scored against a special complexity index. My father tortured his way through the written calculations and finally read out to my mother that his complexity index was 34, hers was 43, and mine 30, but that found-ling 2307's was only 28. 'Only twenty-eight,' he said, while my mother said nothing and saw disas-ter beginning to loom. But disaster stayed its hand, when it turned out that 34, 43, and 30 by comparison with Arnold's 28 wasn't all that serious, although it *was* serious. The letter closed with the words: 'The parental connection of the petitioners to foundling 2307, based on the bacci-form finger patterns, is unlikely, but no more so than the connection to the legitimate child of the petitioners.' The legitimate child of the petition-ers was me. And if you followed the results of the tests, I was just as unlikely to be my parents' child as Arnold was. My parents, on the other hand, insisted that I was certainly their child, so found-ling 2307 must be their child as well, for if their being the parents of 2307 was no more unlikely than their being my parents, then the fact that they were not just probably but actually my parents must mean that they were also definitely or at least almost definitely the parents of Arnold a.k.a. the foundling child. I was confused, I couldn't follow what my parents were saying, and all I could think was that I was in the process of becoming as unlikely as Arnold once had been. But while Arnold was threatening to become more likely with every test, every test was making me less and less likely. I didn't want to become unlikely, I wanted to stay who I was. I didn't want to share with Arnold, not my room and not my food. But I wanted to change places with Arnold even less. Luckily the results of the blood comparisons calmed me down in that the expert opinion stated that I, the legitimate child, was 'possibly and even probably positively' the issue of both my father and my mother, whereas foundling 2307 was 'possibly but not probably positively' the issue of my parents. The 'possible but not probably positive' finding on Arnold increased in my mind to an unmistakable 'highly unlikely'. My parents, who to begin with were depressed by the report, managed over time to construe it to mean 'highly likely' or even 'more or less certain'. My mother in particular allowed time to erode 'possibly but not probably positively' until only 'possibly' was left, and placed all her hopes on the subsequent tests, from which she expected a final confirmation of what was in truth no more than a theoretical possibility of a blood relationship with foundling 2307. Although the responsible youth service that was appointed to represent foundling 2307 advised against further tests by alluding to the probability of negative results, my parents relied on what they perceived as 'overall positive results' to commit to a so-called 'ruling as to anthropological and biological heritage and descent'. To achieve this, all sorts of my parents' and my structural bodily characteristics had to be compared with foundling 2307's, which was first of all time-consuming, and second of all dragged my supposed brother Arnold into the tests as well. The youth service, which was sceptical that the ruling would be positive and wanted to spare its ward a disappointment, told my parents that foundling 2307 had already had to undergo a comparable biological testing as to heritage and that it had come out negative. The boy had had high hopes, and the procedure had left him psychologically scarred. They would therefore only agree to a pictorial comparison; all further tests would have to be approved by the Juvenile Court. The pictorial comparison required photos of my parents, of Arnold, and me. The photo of Arnold in the album was the only one in existence. My mother unstuck it from the album with a heavy heart. If it were to get lost, Arnold in his entirety would be lost too. No usable photo of me existed, so I was sent to the photographer. The photographer owned the only photographic business in town, and was responsible for capturing the likenesses of all the inhabitants. He documented the results of his labours in a showcase, which he had built in front of his shop, and which was one of the fixed stopping points I always aimed for when I was pedalling round town on my bicycle. I played my own form of roulette in front of the showcase, which consisted of making a bet with myself that went 'I bet I know three of the people whose pictures are on display.' Sometimes I raised that to four or five people, but only when I could be sure that the photographer had filled the showcase with class photos or pictures of all that year's first communion or confirmation groups. When the display was nothing but wedding photos or family shots, my chances sank, but often enough I recognized at least one or two people. If I lost my bet, I punished myself with one more ride round town on my bicycle. If I won my bet, I rewarded myself with the same extra ride round town on my bicycle. What I didn't want was ever to appear in the showcase myself. I had always seen the showcase as a kind of pillory that exposed people to the whole world, right at the moment when they thought they'd reached a particular stage in their lives: confirmation, boyfriend/girlfriend, bride and groom, parents with children. I don't know what exposed them, since they were obviously the opposite of exposed, dressed in their best with their hair done. And yet I could see time eating away at them, the children growing up, the parents getting old. When I looked into the showcase of photos, I understood that people have to die. And that wasn't all: I often saw them as already dead: hair styled to death, dressed up to death, photographed to death. I didn't want to be put in the showcase and until now, nobody had had the idea of sending me to have my picture taken. My parents had been perfectly satisfied that bits of me turned up in existing photos, and sometimes almost none of me at all. Now everything depended on my being as clearly visible as possible, which meant, among other things, that I was stuck into a white shirt with an open collar and my father ordered me to get a short haircut that turned me into a sort of inmate of a camp. I was shaved almost bald and then photographed from all sides. The Anthropological Institute that set up the testing had expressly indicated that the ears must be clearly visible and that a picture of the ears from behind would be extremely helpful. To come up with a picture of the back of the ears for the institute, a photo had to be taken of the back of the head, which was particularly demanding for the photographer because this was the first time he'd done one. While he took the front and side shots quite routinely, he went to great pains with the back of my head and took an entire series, all differently lit. I only endured the taking of the regular photographs by turning rigid, but the never-ending photographing of the back of my head was torture, as I felt it was somehow the weakest and least appealing part of my body. A person usually lives with the back of his head without actually being conscious of it or paying it any particular attention. The back of my head was an extremely problematic part of my body to me, because since earliest childhood I had always been trying to let my hair grow over it. I thought the most wonderful thing was to have long hair at the back, and I was happy when it reached my collar or grew down over it. The longer my hair, the better I felt about myself. For my father it was absolutely the opposite: the longer my hair, the unhappier he was with me. If my curly baby hair was allowed to reach almost to my shoulders, the limits of my father's tolerance shrank year by year thereafter by several centimetres. The older I got, the shorter my hair had to be. I had gradually reached matchstick length, and any idea that my hair could touch my ears or my shirt collar was long gone. But as time went by, not even that was enough for my father, some inner gauge had established the limits of his tolerance at front-line-soldiers' or rather camp inmates' hair allowance. It wasn't easy to impose, even the hairdresser pleaded for a 'short stylish cut' from now on and recoiled from the all over head-shave. It was the necessity of having photographs for the tests that first allowed my father to achieve his ideal in hair length and have my head shaved down to the skin all around. The shots of the back of my head certainly number among the most painstaking photos ever taken of me. Whether they influenced the comparative pictorial documentation, I cannot say. After about six weeks a letter reached my parents from the Anthropological Institute working under the instructions of the youth service; Professor Friedrich Keller from Hamburg let it be known that comparison between foundling and child listed in petition was hard since only one photo of child listed in petition was provided, as very young infant, and aforesaid photo still revealed only the most general characteristics of all babies, while on the other hand the area of the ears, which was always exceptionally clearly defined even at that age, was invisible, since child's face was framed in a woollen jacket that completely covered the ears. Only now did my parents notice that little Arnold had been photographed with his ears covered up. Nobody was

thinking about his ears back then, said my
mother. The photo had not been intended for a
forensic examination, but as a memento of the
child's first birthday. Nobody had focused on his
ears, including the photographer. The man had
come with all his equipment from Gostynin, the
chief town in the district, to Rakowiec, where my
parents' farm was, just for this, and had even
brought the white woollen blanket with him, but
he didn't have ears on his mind either. Now they
were missing and were making the investigation
harder, which gave me a certain *schadenfreude*,
since it was finally Arnold's fault that I had had to
undergo the torture of having my whole head
shaved and the back of it photographed. I was
obliged to sacrifice every hair on the back of my
head, while nobody had even bothered about
Arnold's ears. To my mind, Arnold was a case of
'easy come, easy go', but I didn't say it out loud,
because my parents were already crushed by the
first sentences in the report. My mother
especially, who had been able to think of nothing
for weeks but the arrival of the official findings,
went into a kind of state of shock when my father
read her the first sentences. She looked down,

propped her head in her hands, and seemed cut off from all communication. Only a trembling of the head betrayed her agitation. Fortunately the professor's next pronouncements sounded a little less pessimistic; he wrote that my photos and those of my parents 'gave a relatively good insight into the hereditary structure of the family'. Among other things, he could deduce from the photos that both my parents revealed 'a high flat forehead'. In foundling 2307, on the other hand, he detected 'a lower forehead with a pronounced curve', which would have argued against any possible relationship if he had not detected the imprint of this same structure on the Tubera frontalia, as he called them, of the forehead of the 'brother of the child named in the petition', i.e., me. This, according to the professor, could indicate 'a common hereditary structure', although it didn't guarantee it. In addition, Professor Keller noted a 'moderately wide, somewhat slit eyelid formation' and concluded that this slit formation of the lids bore no resemblance to my father's or mine, but did resemble my mother's, which he described similarly as 'moderately wide' and 'somewhat slit'. 'You resemble each other,' my father said to my mother, who finally lifted her head from her hands and looked at him. He read her the section about the eyelid formation again, sat down beside her, put his arm around her, and held her to him. My mother kept silent, but I could see the trembling of her head gradually lessen until it stopped altogether. The comparison of ears that ended the official report came out much less optimistically than had been expected, based on the fact that the foundling's ears were quite different from both my parents' and mine in more ways than one. What struck Professor Keller about foundling 2307 in particular was the 'pronounced inward curvature of the helix'. He further noted 'the lack of protrusion of the helix in the region of the upper curve of the ears', which depressed my parents, although they took it in without saying anything. I, on the other hand, was relieved that no pronounced upper curve of the ears or anything similar had been noted on me. The so-called downward angle of the earlobe in comparison with the overall size of the ear also appeared to be greater in foundling 2307 than it was in my father or my mother's size of the ear. In contrast, the downward angle of my earlobe compared with the overall was not notice-ably different from foundling 2307's, according to the report. In consequence, it was Professor Keller's conclusion that despite some shared fea-tures, it was not possible to speak of a measurable family resemblance in foundling 2307. Thus from the perspective of biological heritage, it was 'highly unlikely' that Arnold, the child named in the petition, was identical with foundling 2307.

With that, for me at least, Arnold died again. As did foundling 2307. Given how unlikely it now was that the foundling was my brother, it was equally unlikely that I would have to share my room with him. I was reassured, also a little disap-pointed, but more reassured than disappointed. It was mostly my mother whom I often caught wiping tears from her face or just sitting at the table, staring into space. Sometimes she would stretch out her arms to me, hug me, cover my head with her hands and press it against her stomach. This would cut off my breath, and I'd begin to sweat, as I felt first my mother's stomach and then my whole mother begin to shake. I didn't want to be squeezed against my mother's stomach, and I didn't want her to shake while I was squeezed against her stomach. But the less I breathed, the more she squeezed me against her, almost as if she wanted to squeeze me right into her stomach. But I didn't want to be squeezed into her stomach, I didn't want to be squeezed, period. My mother had never squeezed me before, and now I didn't want to be squeezed any more, I was doing fine without being squeezed. But my mother apparently didn't do fine any more unless she squeezed me. 'Let me squeeze you,' she said sometimes, out of nowhere. When she squeezed me then, it was a squeeze that was heavy, despairing, and came from a body that shuddered and shook. The more she shook and shuddered, the harder she squeezed me against her belly and almost into it. I didn't dare say to my mother that I didn't want to be squeezed. Sometimes I pulled away from her hands and backed away from her embrace. 'Let me squeeze you,' my mother said, but I bent my knees a little at the last moment and simultaneously took an evasive step backward, so that my mother, eyes half-shut and already in something like a trance, reached into mid-air and almost fell over. Then she caught herself, jerked her eyes open, stared at the empty space that had opened between her and me, and all at once the colour drained from her face. She stood there in front of me pale, like a shadow, as if all the blood had flowed out of her body. While my mother had difficulty recovering from the results of the expert report, my father just spent that much more time with his business. Until now he had been considerate of my mother in every way and had done everything to try to make the search for Arnold successful, but now I often saw him getting into fights with my mother. The fight usually ended with my father having an attack of rage, yelling, slamming doors, and always finishing with the sentence 'I have to take care of the business!' When he took care of the business, it meant first and foremost increasing turnover. Until now he had taken care of the business too, but neglected his business ground rules, which were: 'To stand still is to retreat. And retreat is the beginning of the end.' To forestall that, he decided to build his own cold storage shed. Until now, the meats were stored in a refrigerated facility on the edge of town, which had the disadvantage that the storage cost money. Since every increase in turnover went along with an increase in goods stored, every increase in turnover was also tied up with increased storage fees. To make space for the cold storage shed, the outbuildings by the house had to be pulled down and the garden moved. The outbuildings consisted of the stables of the former coach stop, a washhouse, and a tool shed with a pigeon loft on top. My father called the old, somewhat rickety buildings a 'Polish pigsty'. But he had left them in the state he found them, in part because they reminded him of his past as a farmer in Rakowiec. The stable with its stalls and the iron hooks from which brittle harnesses all covered with powdery mould still hung, the washhouse with its stone cauldron that could be fired directly underneath, the zinc tub that wasn't only for laundry but also served as our family bath, the tool shed with its tools, the rake, sickle, scythe, and the whetstone that had to be used with a treadle. The pigeon loft with a dozen pigeons nesting in it, which my father called by name as he scattered the feed for them, and which seemed to know him. All of it was razed to the ground within a week. First the pigeons were killed, then the stable, tool shed, and washhouse pulled down. The family was given its part to play in the work. My father directed manoeuvres, my mother stood in the wreckage in rubber boots and made herself useful wherever required. My job was to help clear away the rubble. All day long I filled bucket after bucket with building debris and carried it all to the loading point at the entrance to the yard. During the demolition the whole area was covered in dust, and the dust wouldn't clear even when the last remains of the rubble had been loaded onto trucks and driven away. The dust was on your skin, in your clothes, in your mouth, in your eyes. It tasted of straw, dried manure, earth, and animals, and just a little of the feed my father had scattered for the birds in the loft. After the dust had settled, the adjoining garden area was levelled right up to the boundary wall and a beech hedge and prepared for excavation. My father forced the architect and the builders to hurry, and my mother in her own way also seemed in a hurry to get the cold storage shed built. Both slept only a few hours a night at best, since the business had to be kept running. After a few weeks the framingup of the building was celebrated, at the same time as the remaining ground was asphalted over, so that in the future delivery trucks could drive up; and in less than three months from the demolition, on the place where harnesses had once been stored, the stone wash cauldron had been fired up, and we had taken baths in the zinc tub, stood a sort of storage hangar with blue-grey paint and an insulated door with a combination lock, and cold vapour escaped from the door when you opened it. The investment was worth it, and the cold storage shed gained my father a jump on his competitors. He could plan further ahead, organize things on a larger scale, take advantage of price fluctuations, and on top of all that, rent out part of the storage area to the other store owners, who needed refrigerated space but did not have their own facilities. Business flourished to such an extent that with time my father had six delivery trucks and as many drivers under contract to him to pick up orders and deliver them. Most of the time my father was on the road with one of the drivers. He went 'on tour', as he put it. He still operated on the principle that the most important thing was contact with the customers. And if he wasn't visiting customers, he dropped in on the farms and slaughterhouses from which he got his meat. Visits to farms took place mostly at weekends, and quite frequently on Sundays. My father looked after business seven days a week, and seven days a week my mother helped him. One evening when my father had not been out 'on tour', and had spent the day catching up with office work, my mother had a fainting spell and fell so badly on the kitchen floor that she fractured her skull. It took weeks for the fracture to heal sufficiently to allow my mother to take up her daily routine again. But she spent her time in hospital doing nothing but thinking about the past, the war, their flight, and the dreadful thing that was done to her. The skull fracture healed, but after my mother came back from the hospital, she was even more withdrawn, silent, and still. My father tried to cheer her up, he bought her presents, and surprised her by announcing a new car. Without telling my mother or me, he had sold the black limousine with the shark's teeth and ordered a totally new model of car which had never been on the market before, a so-called Opel Admiral. The car allowed him in some way to promote himself from captain to admiral, and he thought he could confer distinction on the family with it too. The car had now reached the dealers, it only had to be paid for and collected. My father wanted to pay cash for the car. He even paid cash for the meat he bought from the farms, and when he was in Rakowiec and went to the cattle market, he had settled his business in cash too. Paying cash was a matter of honour and gave you tangible possession of the things you bought, and a tangible connection to the money you had to sacrifice to buy them. If it had been up to my father, he would have run his entire business on cash. With wages in particular, he would have preferred to pay his drivers at the end of the month in coin in the hand out of a money box, instead of transferring the money to a bank account. He wanted to put the money for the Admiral right into the dealer's hand. It was a fat bundle of hundred-mark notes that he had collected from the bank the day before he bought the car. In the afternoon he deposited the money in an empty cigar box on the kitchen table, and my mother, in her depression, threw it into the kitchen stove that evening before my father could intervene. She

---

didn't want an Admiral, she said. She wanted her child. Then she sat down at the table and didn't say another word; her head just started trembling again, the way it did before. If I had committed this outrage, my father would certainly have beaten me half to death. But he didn't touch my mother. He didn't even yell, just took it in, grabbed the coal tongs, and hauled as many of the burning hundred-mark notes as he could seize hold of out of the fire. He was able to save part of the money, and the bank replaced all the notes that were only partway burnt and were clearly identifiable. The rest, about a third, were lost, but he saved the ashes for a long time in a preserving jar. After this incident, I never heard my father fighting with my mother again. And the burned money was never mentioned again either. He bought the Admiral in spite of it. But the same day the car rolled into the yard and was parked next to the cold storage shed, he composed two letters, one to the appropriate youth bureau and one to the Red Cross search service, proposing a ruling as to anthropological and biological heritage and descent. The search service supported the proposal, but the relevant youth bureau, as it

said in a reply to my parents, wanted to protect
ward number 2307 from further disappointments,
since he had already had to go through a previous
ruling as to anthropological and biological heritage and descent, and, as previously indicated, it
had had a damaging psychological effect on the
boy. In particular the confrontation with the possible parents that had to take place within the
structure of the investigatory procedure had been
very hard on him. Since then, according to the
youth bureau, he had come to terms with his fate,
and a further negative investigation and ruling
would only unsettle him all over again. My father
engaged a lawyer and argued the right on legal
grounds to have a further opinion undertaken.
Foundling 2307's data were already available, my
father's, mother's, and mine were yet to be assembled. The youth bureau agreed to make an
appointment with a Baron von Liebstedt, a doctor
of philosophy and medicine who was professor of
anthropology and biology at the University of
Heidelberg and head of the forensic anthropological laboratory, which would be responsible for
conducting the investigation. Once the appointment for the testing was confirmed to my parents

my mother started to get better. The trembling of her head disappeared, she started to talk more again and even sometimes laughed, she was looking forward to the trip to Heidelberg, and now she even enjoyed the Admiral that would take us there. I did not look forward to the trip. The new car didn't make me happy either, because the moment I sat in it, the symptoms of my travel sickness started up again. I had only to spend the shortest time in the Admiral and I felt queasy, probably from the smell of the car's upholstery. The Admiral was upholstered entirely in artificial materials, the seats covered with artificial leather, the doors and framework with grey artificial fabric, and even the roof of the car was padded with a layer of quilted artificial covering inside. As soon as the car started to move and the engine warmed up, the interior of the car warmed up too and released a sweetish smell from all the artificial fabric that made my nose and mouth and stomach rise in rebellion until within a very short time I was on the verge of throwing up. My father could not understand this physical reaction of mine, he took it as a personal attack and ingratitude. He had worked hard and taken care of our well-being, and by way of thanks I threw up. Luckily I'd been able to avoid throwing up right in the new car till now, but I was worried about a longer drive on the highway. Since my parents also were worried that I wouldn't get through a trip on the highway, they supplied me with pills that I had to start taking several days before the journey. Apparently they worked like an inoculation. I was inoculated against the trip to Heidelberg, and had the feeling that I was inoculated against Arnold too. The pills worked, and I got through the journey without having to throw up once. But the trigeminal neuralgia came back during the journey, which meant that my face was often convulsed with sharp stabs of pain, which produced the grinning cramps that had angered my father before, and this time drove him to rage. This meant that things were pretty tense as we reached the town and went straight to a room in a private boarding house very close to the Forensic Anthropological Institute without looking around Heidelberg at all. Although my father was driving an Opel Admiral, it would never have occurred to him to stay in a hotel. A farmer from Rakowiec didn't go to hotels. A farmer from

Rakowiec also didn't drive an Admiral. But my
father could hardly document the success of his
business in a two-horse carriage. A farmer from
Rakowiec didn't have appointments with a professor who was a doctor of philosophy and medicine
in the normal way of things either, and certainly
not with one who was a baron to boot, and so, for
the very first time next morning I saw this utterly
self-confident man with an attack of something
close to stage fright. My father was as nervous as
an examinee, and my mother tried to calm him
by tying his tie and helping him into his suit and
shoes. She turned the farmer into a businessman,
and he began to shed his unease and insecurity as
he went out onto the street in his proper grey
suit, with a coat and hat, and walked ahead of me
and my mother with a firm stride in the direction
of the forensic laboratory. The laboratory was
located in a complex of buildings made up of
nineteenth-century villas. My father didn't spend
much time looking and aimed straight for the
first building, which turned out not to be the
Institute of Forensic Anthropology but the Institute of Forensic Pathology, which you couldn't
get into without an employee pass. The porter

pointed us toward the Laboratory of Forensic Anthropology, which was on the inner side of the complex; we went in rather hesitantly, since at the very moment we were about to climb the steps leading to the main entrance flanked with columns, a hearse came driving towards us and stopped right in front of the villa. The driver got out, bounded up the steps, and disappeared into the villa. After my father had waited long enough to reassure himself that no corpses were about to be delivered, he went into the building himself. A porter accompanied us to Baron von Liebstedt's workrooms, where a receptionist took down our particulars and then escorted us to a laboratory assistant. We were led into a waiting room and without explanation instructed by the lab assistant to take off our shoes and socks (or stockings), which my mother did in a little changing room, while my father and I did it on the spot. My father, who was no longer the slender young soldier of the old photographs, but an overweight businessman, had trouble bending over, so I had to help him take off his shoes and socks. I had often helped him put on and take off his shoes already, but I had never taken off his socks. I had also, I suddenly realized, never seen my father's bare feet. What I knew of my father was his head, neck, hands, and part of his forearms. I had never seen the rest, and until this moment it had seemed completely natural to me that my father's body was made not of flesh and blood, but of starched shirts, a three-piece suit, and leather shoes. Now I took off his socks in the Institute of Forensic Anthropology of the University of Heidelberg and had to realize that my father's feet were no different from anyone else's, but that, taken each by itself, they were different from one another. My father had two completely different feet. The right foot was fairly fleshy and muscular, with short, powerful toes that made firm, flexible contact with the floor, as did the whole foot. The left foot was narrow, bony, and a little arched, its toes claw-like and just as bony. Curiously the nails on the left foot were not clipped as short as those on the right foot, so that the impression of claws was reinforced. Neither my mother nor my father had ever said anything about my father having two different feet, and even now he declined to notice anything about his feet. He let me hand him his socks, and stuck them in the pockets of his jacket as though this too were obvious, while I arranged the shoes neatly under the chair. Before I had time to think any further about my discovery, the laboratory assistant appeared and announced that she would now begin by taking impressions of our feet. There was still no sign of Professor Liebstedt, and maybe he would only become involved when there were more important things to do than take impressions of feet. I had imagined that taking impressions of your feet would be like taking fingerprints, and was waiting impatiently to see my parents and myself with inky feet. But instead of pressing our feet into ink-pads and then rolling them on a white file card, the laboratory assistant assembled a tub-like container in front of us and filled it with hot, wet, steaming cloths floating in a white plaster brew. The plaster-soaked cloths were wrapped around my father's, my mother's, and my right feet. Apparently the laboratory only needed an impression from one foot each. The laboratory assistant, who busied herself exclusively with our right feet and didn't reward our left feet with so much as a glance, apparently noticed nothing of the enormous difference between my father's left and right feet either. The plaster impression of his right foot would point to a completely different human being from the plaster impression of his left foot, and for one moment I wondered if I should point out this ambiguity to the lab assistant. I didn't, mostly because I was afraid of my father. He was inclined to sudden rages, and besides I had already provoked some upsets during the car trip. Moreover, I told myself, I could play a trick on Arnold *and* foundling 2307 respectively. If I called the lab assistant's attention to my father's feet, then the odds of a family relationship would double. If foundling 2307 didn't have strong fleshy feet with short flat toes, he was sure to have bony arched feet with long curved toes. If both foot impressions from my father were set out, the examiners could choose the foot that fit. But that would make it almost certain that I would have to share my future life with Arnold. I didn't want to share my life with Arnold. I didn't want to share anything with Arnold. So I kept quiet and let fate take its course. The lab assistant was the goddess of fate, and she had chosen Father's right foot. After the plaster dried, the stiffened cloths were taken off us. The cloths, explained the lab assistant, moulded the particular hollow form that would be cast at the next stage in the work. The artificial foot thus obtained could then be measured and assessed minutely in the laboratory. According to the lab assistant, it really wasn't possible to lay the persons under investigation and their respective body parts on Baron von Liebstedt's desk for days on end. The woman, who had until now done her job with a certain severity, reacted to her own words with a bark of laughter, which was suppressed as abruptly as it had erupted. My father took the opportunity to ask the lab assistant about Professor Liebstedt. 'The professor isn't here?' asked my father. 'No,' stated the lab assistant. Then she fell silent, as did my father. Apparently he didn't trust himself to say another word, which might perhaps be explained by the fact that we were still standing there in our bare feet. The lab assistant led us to a foot bath, where we could clean ourselves and get rid of the remaining bits of plaster. After my mother and I had washed our feet, it was the turn of my father's foot. This time it was my mother who helped my father, washing his right foot, and taking charge of drying it and giving it its sock again. After we had dressed, the lab assistant announced that we should strip to the waist. 'To determine the distinctive points of body structure,' she said, 'and please, one after the other'. 'And Professor Liebstedt?' said my now once more fully clothed father in a somewhat firmer tone of voice. 'We have an appointment today. We came just for this.' The lab assistant looked at my father in surprise, clicked her tongue a little, then pursed her lips like a truculent child, walked with exaggerated slowness to her desk, looked at the open diary, and said in a thin voice that we wouldn't even be here without an appointment and that our appointment with the professor was in the afternoon. Foot impressions and distinctive points of body structure were her personal responsibility. Distinctive points of cranial structure would be marked and analyzed by the professor himself this afternoon. 'And now,' said the lab assistant, 'please undress. But one after the other.' As if we were fighting to undress for the lab assistant. Quite the opposite. I stood aside for my father, who stood aside for my mother, who then disappeared with the lab assistant behind a curtain. After my father's distinctive points of body structure had been registered too, I went behind the curtain, took off my shirt and undershirt, and waited. The lab assistant surveyed me with a cool eye and clicked her tongue appraisingly the way she had clicked before. Then she said, 'Let's start,' and put an elastic tape measure round my shoulders, to measure that girth. She noted down the number, put the tape measure round my chest, measured its girth, made notes again, and finally put the tape measure round my stomach. Although the laboratory was quite cool, the whole measuring business had made me feel hotter and hotter. I began to perspire from shame and embarrassment and felt a film of sweat begin to build on my chest, getting wetter and wetter, collecting in the cleft of my breastbone, then trickling down my stomach in thin streams to seep into the waistband of my trousers. When the lab assistant was ready to remove the tape measure from my stomach it was stuck on so tight from the wetness that she had to pull it off my skin like a Band-Aid. The lab assistant held up the wet tape gingerly to read off the measurement. She didn't roll the tape back up, she dropped it in the waste bin. 'Now the Rohrer index,' she said more to herself than to me, picked up a set of wooden calipers with notches and numbers on it, and pinched my stomach with it, which made my stomach muscles contract involuntarily. The calipers slipped off. 'Stomach out,' she said. I let my stomach muscles go again and held my breath at the same time so that the lab assistant was finally able to grab a fold of my stomach with the calipers and hold on. While she kept its grip on the fold with one hand, she reached for her papers with the other and noted down the data that she could read off the calipers. Apparently something struck her as nonsensical even as she was writing it down, so that she concentrated on her notes for some time, without loosening the grip of the calipers one iota. She counted and compared, hesitated and finally corrected her notes while I kept on holding my breath, because the moment I let the slightest bit of air into my lungs and my stomach moved a little, the lab assistant clamped the calipers harder together. So I'd stop breathing again, which meant that the grip relaxed a little. After she'd finished her corrections, she loosened the calipers from my stomach and I was allowed to get dressed. I went and sat down with my parents, who had settled in the waiting room meanwhile, and didn't tell them anything about my experiences with the calipers. My parents seemed quite free and easy; either they didn't want anyone to notice that their stomach folds had been measured too, or they didn't care. After a time the lab assistant appeared in the waiting room and told us we could go to lunch, but admonished us not to be late back on any account and that it would be best if we didn't leave the building at all but had our lunch in the canteen. The lab canteen was on the top floor of the Forensic Anthropology Laboratory and was apparently also used by employees of other institutes. All the tables were taken, so we sat down with a man who was eating alone and was just in the process of pushing away his empty plate and opening a bottle of beer. The man was wearing a black overall, it was the driver of the hearse, who greeted us immediately by saying he'd already seen us outside. He was a non-stop talker, and informed us, without our having asked, that he always had a lot to do at Forensic Pathology, and that he always ate lunch at Forensic Anthropology. He said Forensic Anthropology and not the Forensic Anthropology

Laboratory, which implied that he was really familiar with everything around here. He was really familiar with the different canteens too; besides Forensic Pathology and Forensic Anthropology, he knew the canteens in the Court of Appeals, Forensic Psychiatry, the Regional Tax Office, and the Regional Nerve Clinic. He was around here a lot, it went with his job. Of course he didn't have anything to do with Regional Taxes, professionally speaking, it would be great if he did, he only went there because someone he knew worked there and the two of them sometimes went to the canteen. He used to go to the Regional Tax Office canteen regularly. To be exact, he had gone there almost every day. We wouldn't believe what kind of a canteen the tax officials treated themselves to. Other canteens mostly served liver sausage with fried eggs or something but he hadn't ever seen liver sausage with fried eggs on the tax officials' menu. Chicken fricassee and fried herring, which were almost daily items in other canteens, didn't show up in Regional Taxes either. He at least, in all his time at Regional Taxes, had never eaten liver sausage and fried eggs or fried herring or chicken fricassee. Nor had he ever seen the tax officials eating anything of that sort. The tax officials ate completely different things, veal cordon bleu for example, or cauliflower with brown butter and Prague ham or pineapple baked in sauce with cheese slice and chicory. He had never found cordon bleu in any other canteen, the Regional Taxes canteen was the only one where you could eat cordon bleu, which was more or less his favourite dish. If cordon bleu was on the menu, he ordered cordon bleu. While the man talked, my parents studied the menu, which listed not one of the dishes he had mentioned. Instead there was headcheese with *rémoulade* sauce and fried potatoes or scrag end of pork, also with fried potatoes, which made the choice quite easy. My father dispatched me to the counter where I ordered three scrag ends of pork, which we could collect in a few minutes from the food station. He had had the scrag end of pork too, said the driver of the hearse. Brawn made him uneasy, and when meat was on the menu, he ate meat. My father, who like the rest of us had been silent up till now, said he was the same way. Next time, said the hearse driver, we should eat at Regional Taxes. He wouldn't eat there again himself,

---

because there had been trouble about his hearse.
He'd always parked the hearse in front of
Regional Taxes, which was perfectly normal, all
the other people using the canteen who didn't
have reserved parking space in the courtyard of
Regional Taxes parked their cars in front of
Regional Taxes. But one day there'd been complaints about his hearse that went all the way up
to the director of Regional Taxes. The complaints
came mostly from the Regional tax officials themselves, who felt it didn't look good for the finance
office to have a hearse parked semi-permanently
in front of the building. The image of the tax
offices and of the Regional Tax Office in particular was not altogether the best, and the hearse, as
one of the officials had said to his face, would
cause permanent damage to Regional Taxes'
reputation. On the one hand, everyone might
think people kept dying all the time, which simply
wasn't true. To the best of his knowledge, said the
official, nobody had died *in* Regional Taxes yet.
On the other hand, a hearse had an effect that
was repellent and client-unfriendly. The official
had said client-unfriendly, said the hearse driver,
since if taxpayers were obligated to pay their taxes,

the officials were equally obligated to treat the taxpayers as clients to whom they were offering a service. Naturally, the official had said, the taxpayers wouldn't appreciate this attitude, no matter how friendly everyone was to them. To the taxpayers, tax officials were nothing but bloodsuckers and muggers. He had had to listen to being called both, the tax official had said, and now he and his colleagues didn't want to listen to themselves be called grave robbers as well. The hearse in front of Regional Taxes came close to this, which was why it seemed to him and his colleagues to make a mockery of the work of the tax authorities, which were there only to serve the public good. The hearse driver ended his narration, took another pull from the beer bottle, gave a pregnant smile, narrowed his eyes a little, and said, 'The dead pay no taxes.' Although we didn't really know what he meant by this, my parents smiled at the hearse driver and I did too, while he picked up the bottle, took a long pull as some kind of reward for his accomplishments, put the bottle down again, wiped his mouth, and was silent. My parents and I were silent too, we worked our way through the scrag end of pork until my father

couldn't stand the silence any longer and said to
the hearse driver, 'The last shirt has no pockets,'
which set the latter off into long disquisitions on
the nature of shrouds. The disquisitions consisted
of the fact that there wasn't just the widest imagin-
able choice of shrouds, in both size and materials.
There actually were also shrouds with pockets.
Lots of people would absolutely insist that their
dead had shrouds with pockets, but this always
meant pockets put on afterwards, never pockets
already worked in. The recent fashion was for
monogrammed breast pockets, stitched in black,
of course, and narrow. Some customers would
also stick black pocket handkerchiefs into their
dear departed's breast pockets. White shroud and
black pocket handkerchief, said the hearse driver,
like going to a cocktail party. But the only place
the departed was going was the crematorium,
usually the crematorium in Heidelberg South.
Heidelberg South Crematorium had only been
completed very recently and had the largest
capacity. The director was a good acquaintance of
his, who had once worked in the funeral business
himself and he'd sometimes helped the men out
when there were bottlenecks and taken over

various transports. Black, of course, said the
hearse driver, and gave such a big grin that even
my parents noticed that this must be a particularly
special hearse driver's joke. My parents smiled in
a friendly way, but were no longer really listening.
They both looked as if they'd had enough of the
food and were sleepy. My father's eyes closed for
seconds on end, and my mother just as regularly
stared off into the distance with an exhausted and
simultaneously rather hunted look. I was the only
one still awake, and was watching the hearse
driver closely, which he took to signify a real
interest in his stories. But I was more interested
in his face and the way he looked, trying to find
in them evidence of his occupation. I was searching for death in the hearse driver – or at least the
corpse. Death had a ruddy face and brownish
teeth with a gap in the lower jaw. Its hair was
combed straight back, with no parting, and
reached almost to its collar. The hair was shiny
and obviously had hair cream in it. Death used
hair cream. I didn't like that. I also didn't like the
fact that the man's sideburns had hair cream on
them too. On top of that, he had a big brown
mark on his cheek with a reddish crust on it. I

imagined that the mark must be an age spot. Some people called age spots tomb spots or grave spots, and you could see them most clearly on old people's hands. Even my father already had some of these grave spots on his hands. But not yet any on his face. The scab on the hearse driver's grave spot was quite recent. He'd probably scratched around the mark, perhaps even tried to scratch it away. The hearse driver, who was far too young to have a grave spot this big, was afraid of death, I thought, and furthermore fixated on his cheek, which in turn drove him to keep on with his stories. The special thing about the new crematorium, he said, was the capacity of its ovens. Everything stands or falls by the ovens. If the ovens were no good, the whole crematorium would be no good. The new ovens were absolutely fantastic, his acquaintance the director had once demonstrated the whole works to him and also shown him a collection of unburned and unburnable corpse parts, artificial joints, bits of dentures, metal pins, spikes, clips, and so on. The director had also shown him the remains of a just-cremated corpse. He had opened an ash pan under one of the ovens and taken a few remaining little bones out of the ashes. To show him how perfectly clean and hygienic his cremation ovens were in operation, the director had then put one of the little bones in his mouth and chewed around on it and asked him, the hearse driver, whether he wanted to try it once too. The director had pressed one of the little bones into his hand as he spoke, and kept on chewing around on his bone, saying, 'Try it! Try it!' But he had said thank you, no, said the hearse driver, everything had its limits, although he had absolutely no doubt that the ovens operated completely hygienically. Hygiene was the alpha and omega of cremation systems, said the man, hygiene, tact, and speed were the fundamentals of the business. At the word *business*, my father roused himself from his semi-consciousness, looked at the time, and said that we had to hurry. 'Where do you have to get to?' asked the hearse driver, whose lunch hour apparently went on for several hours. 'To Baron von Liebstedt,' said my father, to which the hearse driver replied with all the confidence of intimate acquaintance, 'And you shouldn't be late.' We got to the laboratory a few minutes late, to be received by the lab assistant with the remark

that we were in her diary for 2 p.m. not 2:10 p.m.
My parents murmured the usual words of apology,
whereupon the lab assistant said that the professor hadn't arrived yet but would certainly be here
any moment. We waited about half an hour for
the professor, who came into the room without
uttering a word of greeting, didn't look at us, and
turned to the lab assistant, who pointed to us with
the words, 'They're here.' The professor turned
round to face us, took a look at my father, my
mother, and me, came over to us, and silently
held out his hand to each of us in turn. Then he
disappeared into his consulting room, we sat
down and we waited again. After another twenty
minutes he appeared, now wearing a white lab
coat, and called us into the consulting room. We
sat down in front of the desk, the professor sat
down behind the desk and leafed through his
documents. He was quite small and finely built,
with a narrow pointed skull, a fringe of grey hair,
and gold-rimmed spectacles. There was a silver
pin on the lapel of his doctor's coat with a V-
shaped symbol, or perhaps it was a 'U'. I didn't
know what this 'V' or 'U' signified, but I thought
it showed that the professor either belonged to

some organization or that he'd earned some special honours. You could tell just from the latter that he was a professor. Besides which he was a baron, which seemed to impress my father even more than his professordom. So nothing could be more wonderful for my father than the professor looking up after an extended perusal of the documents and saying to him, 'You came from Rakowiec, in the district of Gostynin?' Before my father could even respond, the professor said that in contrast to his father's side of the family, who'd lived in Russia, his grandfather on his mother's side also came from Gostynin and had owned a large property there, but that this property was lost, like everything else. At least for the moment. My father, taking heart from this common bond, said, 'The soil was good in Rakowiec, good soil for wheat,' to which the professor said that soil was as good as the people who worked it. His family would certainly have got something out of any soil, whereas the Russians would ruin it. My father looked rather startled and my mother also shrank back a little, because nothing had been said about the Russians till now, and both of them seemed rather unwilling to talk about their experiences with the Russians. 'In Rakowiec we only had dealings with Poles,' said my father. 'In Rakowiec II.' But he came from Rakowiec I, which was right next to Rakowiec II and was a pure German settlement, whereas Rakowiec II was a pure Polish settlement. Rakowiec I had been settled by his forefathers and made arable, and after the former marsh had been turned into a fertile landscape, the Poles had arrived as well and settled Rakowiec II. That had been a fiasco, said my father. While you could see from a long way off that Rakowiec I was a German village, you could also see from a long way off that Rakowiec II was inhabited by Poles. Nothing but cabbages and beets. Garbage in the gardens, mud holes in the streets, gaps in the fences, gaping stalls, geese and hens loose all over the village. In the end the Polish farmers of Rakowiec II were reduced to such poverty that they had to hire out as labourers for the Germans in Rakowiec I. All because of the fiasco. 'You couldn't,' said the professor, who had been fussing with his documents during all this, 'even use the Russians as labourers.' He didn't say any more, but lit a cigarette, which he took from a leather-covered metal case, and leafed through documents again. After some minutes of further study of the dossier he looked up and said he had foundling 2307's footprint data here in front of him, which now had to be compared with our footprint data. 'Our lab assistant will do it today, we'll know more tomorrow.' Now he must concentrate on the area of the head, and would like to begin right away. First the professor examined my parents, while I waited in the waiting room. From this vantage point I could watch the lab assistant, working away at the foot casts that had been poured meanwhile. Apparently there were no other appointments set today for others of the lab's clientele, and she could devote herself to our case. My father's right foot, my mother's right foot, and my right foot were standing in front of her on the table. She was in the middle of painting the sole of my father's foot, along with the toes and heel, with some sort of dark blue ink-like solution. Then she held the painted foot like a stamp in her hand and pressed it onto a big white sheet of paper. She looked at the result of her labour and was quite obviously pleased with it, as she now picked up my mother's foot and then finally mine. Both my mother's foot and my foot caused more problems. She couldn't use either of them just as a stamp, but after applying repeated coats of the solution had to make separate imprints of the different parts of the feet. If she'd chosen my father's left foot with the higher arch as her model, she wouldn't have been able to just simply press it onto the paper like a stamp either. So in case of doubt, I thought, the lab assistant prefers to make her plaster impressions from flat feet, because it makes her work easier. Which also means, naturally, that foundlings with flat feet have an overall better chance of being identified as having a blood relationship with other people. It followed that with my feet, which took more after my father's high-arched, crooked foot, I would have less chance of being reunited with my parents. Fortunately I was not a foundling. Fortunately number 2307 was the foundling, and I could still always hope that foundling 2307 also had feet that were more high-arched and crooked than flat and fleshy. After my parents had come back and sat down in the waiting room again, I was summoned into Professor Liebstedt's consulting room. The professor was sitting behind his desk, smoking. This time he wasn't digging around in his papers, he was staring blankly through the open window into the undimmed brightness of the afternoon. Wreaths of smoke were curling in front of his face and through the smoke I saw that the gold rims of his spectacles had caught a ray of sun and were throwing tiny pinpoints of light up onto the consulting-room ceiling. I lifted my head to watch the tiny lights and became aware that the ceiling apparently hadn't been repainted for years and the old paint had turned grey-brown and was hanging off the ceiling in big patches. Some of the patches seemed to be attached by no more than a thread and threatened to land sooner or later on the professor's head. I also discovered half a dozen holes in the ceiling that looked like little craters and reminded me of bullet holes, although I'd never seen bullet holes before. 'They're bullet holes,' said the professor suddenly, who was no longer looking out of the window but looking at me looking at the ceiling. 'From the war,' he added, 'but that has nothing to do with it.' Then he got up from his chair, came over to me, stroked the back of my head, said the place must have been badly renovated, then said I seemed to be an alert little fellow, perhaps a little too much baby fat, as he knew from his lab assistant, and as you could see anyway. He stroked the back of my head again, and the stroking gradually turned into some sort of measuring of the back of my head, so that it finished with him no longer stroking me but pressing his fingertips hard against my skull and simultaneously palpating bumps and swellings on my head with his thumb. I felt a bit faint under the professor's hand, particularly as his grip was far stronger than you would have guessed from his slight build. He palpated my head with one hand and smoked with the other. Eventually he put out the cigarette and began to palpate my skull with both hands. I had never had the feeling before that I had bumps and swellings in my skull and now I had the feeling that my skull was nothing but. The longer the professor went on palpating, the more bumps and swellings my skull grew, and the longer he went on palpating, the more ashamed I felt of these bumps and swellings. And I began to get hot and sweaty from shame and embarrassment, just as I had that morning during the measuring of my body. This time, however, I wasn't sweating from the chest and stomach, but from my head. And the more my head sweated, the more ashamed I was that the professor had my wet sweaty head in his hands. But he didn't appear to notice. He ended the palpation of my head, washed his hands without saying a word, dried them, jotted down a few notes, and then began to measure my head. For this he picked up a pair of wooden calipers that were marked with a scale of figures, just like the ones for stomach fat, but that opened much wider. He set the calipers once from the front and once from the side, jotted down the measurements, and then reached for another instrument that looked like a screw clamp, which determined what he called the relative width of the angle of the jaw. 'The relative width of the angle of the jaw,' said the professor as he tightened my upper jaw in the screw clamp, 'can be the decisive factor. If the relative width of the angle of the jaw matches, then most often the width of the forehead, the width of the cheekbones, the width of the ears, and the width of the nose, even sometimes the length of the bridge of the nose match too.' I was flattered that the professor was initiating me into his professional secrets, but said nothing, and concentrated all my attention on the pain caused by the two screws that were attaching the screw clamp to my jaw. I deduced from the professor's remarks that width of forehead, width of cheek-bones, width of nose, and width of ears were all going to get measured too. Luckily the screw clamp was only involved for width of forehead and width of cheekbones, while nose and ears were determined with an elastic measuring tape and a contraption like a pair of compasses. The thing like compasses was fitted with two rubber burls instead of a metal point, so it could be set on the skull completely painlessly. The measuring of my nose and ears also went off quite painlessly and only took a few minutes. His work completed, the professor released me into the waiting room where my parents, all dressed and ready in their hats and coats, were waiting for me. As we left the institute, I told my parents how painful the screw clamp fixed on my jaw had been, but they didn't react. I would have liked to have a little sympathy, but nobody sympathized with me. Only when I added that the professor had stabbed me in the face with a pair of compasses did my mother become frightened, and examined my face for puncture wounds or traces of blood. Naturally the examination turned up negative, so there was nothing left for me but to tell my parents that there had been shooting in the professor's consulting room. This remark didn't get any reaction either, except for my father hissing, 'That's enough!' I shut up and followed my parents, who wanted to spend the rest of the day sightseeing in the city. Because the laboratory was on the north bank of the river, we crossed a bridge which my mother said was well known for its noticeable swaying. She got this information from a city guide she had received from the landlady of our boarding house. The bridge turned out to be a massive stone bridge, built of huge, weathered, brown-stained blocks, and it didn't seem to sway at all. We stopped at the apex of the bridge and looked at the river. While I was still on spy alert for any swaying of the bridge, I saw my father put his arm around my mother's shoulders and she bent her head a little so that her cheek was resting on my father's shoulder. I had never ever seen my mother bend her head like this, and for some reason it made me sad. I banished my sadness by jumping in the air several times and landing as hard as I could, to make the bridge start swaying after all. I wouldn't have minded at all right then if the bridge had collapsed. But it didn't. It didn't even sway. Not the slightest movement to be felt. My parents paid no attention to my antics and were walking on. At the end of the bridge they stopped to look at a monument that was a statue of someone called Karl Theodor, according to the city guide, who was also known as the Father of the Pfalz, and whose base was being besieged by the river gods Rhine, Danube, Mosel, and Isar. I took a closer look at the river gods and would have loved to stick the stomach-fat calipers on the naked, prostrate river god Rhine, to determine his Rohrer index. Oddly enough, the river god had a deep furrow on his nose, which ran the length of his nose bone right to the tip, and I imagined that someone had measured the length of the god's nose bone and used the wrong instrument. I reckoned the nose bone was about eight inches long, which was quite a lot, and hurried to catch up with my parents, who hadn't been interested in the river gods and had gone on ahead. 'The Rhine has a furrow down his nose,' I reported to my parents. When they didn't react, I added that the Rhine's nose bone was about eight inches long. My parents still said nothing and turned into a lane that led to the castle. I made a game of running up the lane in a zigzag, but always came tacking back to my parents in between and walked so close behind them that when they looked around they couldn't see me. When I was hiding in their lee, I heard my mother say to my father that it wasn't always easy for 'him' meaning me, either, to which my father said that it wasn't easy for any of us, but 'he' meaning me, still had things the easiest. I'd heard enough and resumed my zigzag course, so that by the end I'd covered three times the distance and was accordingly out of breath. I can't remember very much about visiting the castle, because the whole time my father's words kept running through my head. If I'd always proceeded from the belief that things were hardest for me, my father was proceeding from the belief that they were easiest for me. Things weren't easiest for me. If things were easiest for anyone, they were easiest for Arnold. He didn't have to clean up, he didn't have to do any household chores, he didn't have to be an alert little fellow, and my parents still worried about him the whole time. When my mother was sad, she was sad about Arnold. When my father went to Heidelberg, he went to Heidelberg because of Arnold. And when we visited the castle now, we were only doing it because of Arnold. The castle turned out to be a ruin, which my father identified immediately as a war ruin. 'But it wasn't a bomb,' said my mother, who'd been studying the city guide, 'it was artillery shells.' 'War is war,' said my father, who had had enough of the castle and wanted to start home. We were back in the boarding house before my mother discovered that we'd missed the castle wine cellar and a particularly large barrel that was on exhibition inside. 'Next time,' said my father, but we all knew there wouldn't be a next time. My parents had never taken a trip, and I had never taken a trip either. The trip to Heidelberg, which was to last three days in all, was the only extended trip I ever took with my parents. My parents didn't travel. Because of the business, they said. But the truth was they didn't travel because of their escape. Admittedly the escape hadn't been a trip, but all trips seemed to remind them of the escape.

A farmer from Rakowiec doesn't abandon his house of his own free will. He who abandons his house commits a sin. He who abandons his house is ambushed by the Russians. He who abandons his house will have his house plundered and destroyed. We would start home next day and never see the big barrel, I knew it. We wouldn't cross the bridge with the river gods again either. Before we set off on the trip back, we went to the Forensic Anthropology Laboratory again to find out the results of the tests on our feet. The results of the tests on our heads and build would be forwarded to us in writing later. This time we were punctual, but it wasn't the lab assistant who received us but Professor Liebstedt himself. He led us into the consulting room where three chairs were set out in front of his desk. We sat down, the professor sat down, picked up the leather-covered cigarette case, then thought better of it, put it down again, opened a briefcase with documents and said that the foot comparisons really were quite good. In any event, according to the professor, who was looking at my father, my mother had a pronounced pointed metatarsus positioned towards the outer edge of the foot, and the balls of her big toes showed strongly separated and pronounced vertical creases, whereas the balls of my father's big toes showed a large disc-shaped whorl and a small-whorled core. The legitimate son, on the other hand, by which he meant me, while he looked at my mother, showed a spiral whorl and had no triradius. Foundling 2307 had no triradius either, but both my parents had one. Professor Liebstedt's observations made me conclude that my feet looked the same as foundling 2307's feet, but didn't look the same as my parents'. I had no triradius, the foundling had no triradius, whatever a triradius was. But I also looked the same as Arnold, particularly Arnold's photo, which forced me to realize that the circle around me, Arnold, and foundling 2307 was growing tighter. If I looked the same as Arnold and the foundling, then Arnold and the foundling looked the same as each other. But if Arnold and the foundling looked the same as each other, then we'd soon have another mouth in the house to feed. Now everything came down to how the foundling's and my father's feet had compared. The foot comparison had tested positive for the foundling and my father. The foundling, according to the professor, like my father had a disc-shaped whorl on the balls of his big toes. In addition, my father not only had a broad foot, he also had a clearly defined, broad metatarsus that went with foundling 2307's broad feet and broad metatarsus. 2307's good luck, I thought, Father's right foot goes with his feet. For a brief moment I was sorry I hadn't pointed out the difference in my father's feet to the lab assistant. Now it was too late. My parents were delighted with the positive results; during the professor's remarks my mother had taken hold of my father's hand and squeezed it several times. Now all they wanted to know was the final result of the foot studies, because not even my parents could make much of big-toe curves and large disc whorls. 'Baron,' said my father, 'what does it mean?' 'It means', said the professor, 'that a relationship with the foundling can by no means be ruled out.' 'Although', he went on, 'a relationship cannot be deduced with certainty from the foot studies.' He paused, lit a cigarette, drew on it deeply, and then said with a little smile, as he blew out the smoke: 'Inconclusive, you might say.' Then he stood up, and before my father or my mother could say a word, held out his hand to my parents and me, announced that the results still outstanding would be sent on, wished us a good journey home, accompanied us to the door, and as if to console us, called after us down the stairwell, 'We'll know more when we've evaluated the distinguishing points of cranial and bodily structure.' My parents said very little to each other on the drive home, and the longer they drove, the more aware they became that they were still right where they'd started. Shortly before we left the highway to do the last stretch on the local road, my father was attacked by a kind of fit of rage that gave him chest pains so that he had to stop the car. My mother took his place at the wheel and tried simultaneously to calm my father, who despite his chest pains was ranting about what he described as our totally superfluous trip to Heidelberg. 'Inconclusive,' he cursed to himself, 'inconclusive, you might say.' It had been an utter waste of time, a waste of time and a waste of money. My father didn't stop cursing until my mother turned in at the entrance to our yard, and had to brake for a moment, because there stood the green Volkswagen belonging to Mr Rudolph, the local policeman.

Mr Rudolph told my parents that the cold storage shed had been broken into the previous night and robbed. Almost all the stocks of meat and sausage had been stolen, and on top of that, the thieves had switched off the refrigeration so that everything that wasn't taken had been damaged and might even be totally spoiled. While my mother more or less kept control of herself and said that the insurance people would have to be notified first thing tomorrow because of the claim for spoilage, my father turned white, clutched at his chest again, and would have collapsed that very moment if Mr Rudolph hadn't caught him. He and my mother got my father into the house and got hold of the doctor on emergency call, who diagnosed a circulatory problem, gave my father an injection, and ordered bed rest. My father endured the bed rest for exactly an hour and a half, then he appeared in his bathrobe in the kitchen, where my mother was preparing supper for us and Mr Rudolph too, and confessed to my mother that the contents of the cold storage were not insured. The insurance wouldn't take effect until the first of next month. He'd postponed it a little to save on the premium. For years

---

he'd thrown money down the throats of one insurance company after another and had never had to make a claim. And now this. He sat down, was drenched in sweat again, and gasped for air. My mother didn't know what to do other than call the emergency doctor again, who now seemed very concerned and arranged for my father to be brought into the hospital emergency room. My mother went with my father to the hospital. Mr Rudolph promised her to look after me and to be sure I didn't go to bed too late. I was glad that the man in the green uniform wanted to look after me. It's true that he was a policeman, but he was a much friendlier man than my father. Mr Rudolph talked to me as if I were a grown-up and when I asked him, he explained his radio to me and showed me his service pistol, which he wore in a leather holster attached to his belt. My father didn't talk to me, and he would never have explained the radio to me or showed me the service pistol. Nor would he ever have laid the table the way Mr Rudolph did now and eaten supper alone with me. After we'd eaten the scrambled eggs my mother had cooked, I asked Mr Rudolph all about the break-in at the cold storage shed. They had no proof, he said, but detectives had been there right away next morning and had secured the evidence. They had found fingerprints, but naturally these fingerprints could also belong to the drivers or my parents or even me. 'Even me?' I got a fright, and suddenly imagined I'd done it. I felt guilty, even though I knew it was completely mad. And yet still a voice inside me said, 'I broke into the cold storage shed.' I had also wanted to make the stone bridge in Heidelberg fall down. The bridge hadn't fallen down. And I hadn't broken into the cold storage shed. And yet I still hoped my finger-prints weren't on the cold storage shed door. Had they found any footprints? I asked. Not as far as he knew, said Mr Rudolph. He also didn't think that anyone had looked on the asphalt for footprints. So I explained to him that the best way to get footprints was with wet cloths soaked in plaster. At least that's how they did it in Heidelberg. Mr Rudolph listened to me closely, so I told him about the feet on the lab assistant's desk as well, and the bullet holes in the profes-sor's room and the hearse driver and the little human bones, and I went on telling him for so long that I nearly fell out of my chair with sleepiness. I went to bed and was told next morning that my father didn't have any circulation problems, he'd had two heart attacks and was now in intensive care. My mother was staying at the hospital and only came home to give me my meals. In the evening she made scrambled eggs like the night before and went back to the hospital. Shortly before I wanted to go to bed, Mr Rudolph arrived and said he was taking me to the hospital, my father wasn't doing well. I went to the hospital in the police car and couldn't decide whether I'd rather be a criminal or a policeman. Mr Rudolph came with me all the way to the door of my father's room, but I went in on my own. The invalid was lying on the bed under a tangle of tubes and leads, and my mother was sitting silently beside him. When I leaned over him he looked at me with cloudy, yellowish, watery eyes, but he didn't recognize me. The room was warm and smelled of sweat, medicines, and disinfectants, and before I could exchange even a word with my mother I felt sick and had to leave the room. My mother called for a nurse, who gave me something bitter-tasting to drink. Mr Rudolph took me home. He let me off at the front door and was going back to the hospital. I went to bed alone and was awakened around two o'clock in the morning by a solemn-faced and pale Mr Rudolph with the words that my father had died. Then he laid a Bible on my bedside table and said I should read something, he had to go and look after my mother again. I picked up the Bible, it was as heavy as a stone, and I picked it up not just because of Mr Rudolph but also because of my father. It was the first and only time I ever read the Bible on my own and of my own free will. But the Bible was a thick book, with hundreds of pages, and I didn't know where I was supposed to begin and where I was supposed to stop. But I wanted to be a good son and I didn't dare put the Bible down. I opened it at the page with the heading 'Where do I find it?' I looked for the word Death. I found the word Death without having to look very far. The Bible was full of death, an unending list of pages referred to death. There was physical death and spiritual death, there was the conquest of death and eternal death. There was the kingdom of the dead and the Dead Sea. The most interesting one was the Dead Sea, which I found on a map right at the back of the Bible. The Dead Sea was dark green, whereas the Mediterranean was light blue. I floated on the dark green water of the Dead Sea. I didn't need to move, the waves held me up, the waves rocked me, I had a warm feeling in my veins, I closed my eyes and slept. When I went into the kitchen next morning, I was embraced by my mother, in floods of tears and dressed all in black. Her embrace made me feel as embarrassed as her black clothes did. It took me a few minutes to remember what had happened. Luckily the house really filled up with neighbours, acquaintances, and relatives, giving my mother and me their condolences and offering their help in dealing with the formalities. So we were never all alone in the days that followed, and the sudden silence caused by my father's absence was softened a little. The day of the funeral came closer, and my mother alternated between hectic activity and silent tears of despair. Her black clothing still disconcerted me, but I was even more disconcerted by a black band that my mother slipped over my arm and that I had to wear from now on. None of my school friends

had a band like that, nor any of the teachers. I
was ashamed of the black band, I wore it like a
blemish, and I had the feeling that my school
friends were somehow a little shy of me, and
didn't draw me into their games and teases and
scuffles the way they had before. My school
friends avoided me, I had death on my arm,
death was an illness, it was catching, and nobody
wanted to catch it from me. Whereas my mother
wore her black clothes for a whole year, I was
allowed to take the black band off again after my
father's funeral, so the day of the funeral was a
nice day for me too. But before that, it was time
to say goodbye once more. My father lay on a
bier in an underground room of the cemetery
chapel, where my mother and I could look at him
one last time. We got into the black limousine,
drove to the chapel, and a man in rubber boots
and a green apron took us to him. My mother
threw herself onto the corpse, which lay in its
coffin on a stone platform, embraced him and
kissed him, and then said a prayer by his side that
I couldn't hear and that went on for a long time.
I stood a little way off, I was shivering in the
whitewashed room, and I longed for the day

when I wouldn't need to wear the black band any more. I saw the barred cellar window just above floor level that let in a feeble amount of light. I thought about the man in the rubber boots and the green apron. I saw my father lying under a white shroud, and he still seemed to be breathing, for the white cloth rose and fell before my eyes. I told myself the movement of my father's chest was an illusion, which came from the fact that I'd never seen a person not breathing, and was somehow determined to see every person as a breathing person. At the same time it dawned on me that I'd never perceived my father in his lifetime as a person whose chest and stomach wall rose and fell ceaselessly. And now when he was dead and his breath had stopped, all I could see was a father who never stopped breathing. If I'd stayed with my dead father for longer, a few hours or a whole day, I would certainly have learned to see him as a dead father, not breathing, a totally dead person. But this way I didn't, and for example the white bandage wrapped around his head and under his chin made you think more of somebody who'd been wounded rather than somebody who was really dead. But a wounded man would not have been the cause of my having to wear a black armband. Before we left the chapel, my mother threw herself on my father a second time, kissed him and embraced him even more tenderly than before, and in such an intimate way that I remembered how the two of them had stood on the old Heidelberg bridge. My mother stroked my father's cheeks, she touched the white bandage around his head, she stroked his hair, and finally squeezed his worn, now slightly sallow hands. Suddenly we heard a rustling, my mother jumped in fright, I jumped in fright, the man in the apron and the rubber boots was standing in the doorway and had apparently been standing there for some time. 'We're closing,' he said. He held a bunch of keys in his hand and led us as far as the iron door that opened directly onto the cemetery. Next day we drove in the freshly polished Admiral that was now an evil-grinning hearse to my father's funeral, where I was surprised to discover how many people paid their last respects. Alongside our neighbours and relatives were representatives of the butchers' guild, the distributors' association, the rifle club, the local chamber of trade

---

and industry, and the church congregation, which showed me that my father was a highly regarded man. They all listened to the pastor's funeral sermon, which ended with organ music and the brief, cold tolling of the funeral bell. My mother and I went out of the cemetery chapel in front of everyone else and followed six black men in tail-coats and top hats, one of whom I recognized as the man with the green apron. The men carried the coffin to the graveside and used three thick ropes to let it down into the earth. A brass band played a funeral march, the pastor said a prayer, the riflemen lowered their heavy club flag over the coffin, and finally first my mother and then I went to the open grave and threw a spadeful of earth onto the coffin. As I stood with the spade in my hand and looked at the massive slab of oak under which my father lay, I had the feeling I had to prevent any last blow from reaching him. I turned the spade a little and let the earth trickle down past the edge of the coffin. I didn't want to throw earth on my father. I wanted to be his good, sad son, and I thought about how I was surely suffering over my father's death, but couldn't feel that I was suffering, and that as soon as the coffin was all covered with earth, I'd be allowed to take the black band off my arm.

From the day of the funeral, my mother took over my father's business. She was just as strict as my father had once been. The drivers called her Chief, the suppliers respected her, the customers revered her, and nobody noticed how deeply she suffered over everything that had happened. It was only in the evenings, after the drivers had left the yard and the big searchlight was switched on that bathed the cold storage shed in dazzling light every night after the robbery, that my mother became herself again. But when she became herself again, she wasn't a chief, she was a woman who vanished in a fog of grief. She took care of me but she didn't seem to notice me, and if she did notice me it was as if she wasn't seeing me, but somebody else. Often when she looked at me she was overcome by emotion. She gazed at me, her eyes lost themselves in my face, and while her eyes lost themselves in my face, her own face seemed to blur and dissolve. These moments were torture for me, I moved my mother and I didn't want to move her. Nobody else reacted to the sight of me this way. I was too fat, I was on the verge of puberty, and I had a short haircut, even though it hadn't been trimmed since my father died. There was nothing about me that was moving in any way at all. Most people overlooked me, and the ones who didn't overlook me told me to go to the hairdresser, eat less, and do more sport. Only my mother was so moved by the sight of me that her face almost seemed to dissolve when she looked at mine. My moved and dissolved mother made me bad-tempered and uneasy. I could feel that she saw something in me that she had lost. I reminded her of my father. And I also reminded her of Arnold. But I couldn't take the place of Arnold for her. If it had been up to me, I would have taken Arnold's place for her without further ado. I could eat for two. Watch TV too. I brought enough bad reports home from school already. No Arnold was needed in that department. But I wasn't enough for her. I was only what she didn't have. I was the finger in the wound, the grain of salt in the eye, the stone in her heart. In the most literal sense of the phrase, I was to weep for, but only much later did I understand why. Back then all I noticed was that the sight of me put a look of pain on my mother's face, and that I began to hate this pain as much as I hated my own reflection in the mirror. I became what is known as a difficult boy, ungrateful, obstinate, always irritated, always pestering my mother just when she felt bad. Luckily Mr Rudolph continued to take care of my mother and me too. Mr Rudolph dealt sensitively with my mother's pain and didn't take offence at my nastiness. Mr Rudolph got my mother's permission for me to wear my hair long. In exchange I promised him not to be so irritable with my mother. Aside from this he helped my mother with procedures with the authorities and all sorts of formalities – and he gave her records of operettas. Before my father's death my mother had never heard records of operettas. A farmer from Rakowiec doesn't listen to operettas. A farmer from Rakowiec listens to the cows in the stall, the wind on the fields, and the ringing of the church bells. With Mr Rudolph she was able to give herself over to her love of *Land of Smiles* and *The Gypsy Baron* for the first time. When my mother listened to operettas with Mr Rudolph, she always did so on Sunday afternoons and never behind closed doors. I was always allowed to go into the living room filled with music, and I never saw any kind of intimacy between them. Mr Rudolph sat in the armchair with a cup of coffee and a piece of cake and listened to the music. My mother sat on the sofa and listened too. I ate my cake and ran through the house and whenever I came back into the room, they were sitting where they'd been sitting before. Only once did I see that my mother had tears in her eyes and Mr Rudolph was in the process of passing her a handkerchief but quickly pulled it back as I came into the room. I didn't know what had happened, but I noticed that Mr Rudolph now visited my mother during the week more often than before, to help her with some kind of written procedures. One day she revealed to me that Mr Rudolph had offered to support her in the further search for Arnold, for which she was extremely grateful. The results of the comparative tests of cranial and body structure still hadn't come in, and despite a letter of reminder she still had had no reply. Mr Rudolph had now weighed in in his official capacity and immediately heard back that the test results had indeed not yet been sent out, but would be sent out immediately. It was only a few days before my mother had the letter from Baron von Liebstedt in her hand, enclosing a voluminous number of pages with the heading 'Anthropological-Biological Heritage Findings re Foundling 2307'. My mother asked Mr Rudolph to read out the findings. The pages contained the information that the shape of the cranium in both my mother and my father was considerably rounder when measured longitudinally and laterally than in foundling 2307, but that my measurements both longitudinal and lateral were not dissimilar to those of foundling 2307. In addition the cheekbones were wider in the adults than in foundling 2307 and me, but this, according to the findings, also had to do with fat deposits. I had never heard words like *fat deposit* before and ran my hands over my face as unobtrusively as possible to reassure myself that I didn't have any. Besides, I had no idea where the cheekbones were located and was forced to discover that my cheeks seemed filled with what the professor called fat deposits. I suspended my self-examinations and started listening to Mr Rudolph again, who was now informing us that the relative height of the forehead was much greater in the man than in the woman, the child, and the foundling, but that due allowance had to be made in the measurement for developing baldness. Then the findings moved on to discuss the relative angle of the jaw, and I remembered the painful screws that had compressed my jaw into the screw clamp. Given what it had cost me, it was rather disappointing that the findings concerning the relative angle of the jaw only took up a single sentence. The sentence ran, 'The relative angle of the jaw shows little differentiation.' This even stopped Mr Rudolph, who looked up from the paper and asked, 'Differentiation from what?' I didn't know, my mother didn't seem to know either. And perhaps she didn't care, because the whole time Mr Rudolph had been reading out the findings, she'd seemed to be somewhere else. Before she'd always been extremely tense when a new report or even a simple letter from one of the authorities involved in the search for Arnold arrived, but now the professor's papers didn't seem to interest her any more. Even the information that the Rohrer index was higher in my parents than in foundling 2307 didn't interest her very much. And besides,

Professor Liebstedt qualified this by stating that the man and the woman were somewhat fatter than the foundling but that this could be explained by the difference in age. The married couple, according to the professor, had ample adipose tissue, with very prominent stomachs. The legitimate son of the married couple, meaning me, also had ample adipose tissue, though his stomach was less prominent, but this was a consequence of the difference in age. Foundling 2307, in contrast, was somewhat lacking in adipose tissue. So Arnold was thin. I on the other hand was fat. I didn't like the professor's findings. I also didn't like it that he described my less prominent stomach as less prominent only because I was younger than my parents. Although this result argued against a relationship between my parents and foundling 2307, my mother still didn't seem all that troubled by it. I, on the other hand, was certainly troubled that foundling 2307 gave evidence of a different body structure, and I would have preferred it if my parents and I had taken over the thin part and the foundling the fat part. I didn't like the distinctive features of the back of the head much either, as the findings declared the back of my head to be more convex than that of my parents, whereas the back of foundling 2307's head was only somewhat convex, which was neither much of a resemblance nor a difference. In addition, the professor had noted protuberances of the forehead in both me and the foundling, whereas he had noted less prominent protuberances of the forehead in my parents. That spoke against me in more ways than one. First, I didn't find it particularly flattering to have prominent protuberances in my forehead, and second, it made me resemble foundling 2307. Things were a little more propitious when it came to the shape of the nose, which was apparently pronouncedly convex in both my parents and me, and pronouncedly concave in the foundling. As for the length of the nose bone, the finding was simply, 'The length of the nose bone is largish in all subjects.' This was followed by the sentence, 'The lower part of the nose is not prominent.' I wasn't the only one puzzled; Mr Rudolph also got stuck on this point. Neither of us had known until now that a person had a lower part of the nose, and we needed to get used to this fact. Mr Rudolph didn't allow himself to be diverted for long and strove to stick to reality since he knew what was at stake for my mother. So without further interruption he reported the further description of the distinctive features of the nose, which Professor Liebstedt called the flare of the nostrils. He characterized the flare of my mother's nostrils and the foundling's as moderately pronounced with a strong upward arc, whereas the flare of my nostrils and my father's were overly pronounced with an inverse arc. Inconclusive, so to speak, is what Professor Liebstedt would have said. I kept quiet for the time being and went on listening to the findings, which were now taken up with the nostrils, including both the shape of the nostrils and the visibility of the inner walls of the nostrils. While the shape of the nostrils in all participants was of medium size with an underdeveloped septum, only the inner walls of foundling 2307's nostrils were clearly visible, whereas they were not clearly visible in my parents or me, a piece of news that gave me a certain satisfaction. The investigation of distinctive features of mouth, chin, and ears had given rise to quite differing results. The fullness of the lips in my mother and the foundling was very pronounced, whereas it was less pronounced in my father and me. And the foundling's full lower lip displayed a so-called 'strong outward tilt for much of its length', which was not evident in my mother's equally full lower lip. The indentation in my father's upper lip departed from the indentation in mine, but not my mother's. The indentation of my father's upper lip was certified as shallow, my mother's as medium, mine and the foundling's as deep. Lucky none of us has a harelip, I thought to myself, for where there's a deep indentation of the upper lip, there's the possibility of a very deep indentation of the upper lip. And from a very deep indentation of the upper lip it was no big jump to a harelip. One of my schoolmates had a harelip, and I knew that this meant being tormented day after day. A harelip was far worse than a prominent stomach or protuberances on the forehead and I wouldn't have wished a harelip even on Arnold. The examination of chin and ears hadn't achieved any real clarity either, and the more detailed the findings, the more confusing they got. Nevertheless Mr Rudolph read on undistracted, maybe it wasn't so confusing for him, and besides, he was used to official reports and documents from authorities. My mother on the other hand seemed completely lost in thought, glancing up only occasionally, to show Mr Rudolph she was still listening. But I could tell that she was pre-occupied by more than upper lips and lower noses. Only when Mr Rudolph said that he was coming to the results of the report that were listed at the end of the text did my mother start paying a little more attention. The so-called 'summary conclusion' of the findings was, logically, just as unclear as the examination of the individual dis-tinctive features of the body. So the conclusion concerning distinctive features of the mouth was that my mother's parental kinship was apparently marginally positive, while my father's parental kinship was extremely unlikely. As regarded the distinctive features of body structure, by contrast, Professor Liebstedt declared the parental kinship of the married couple to be moderately unlikely. You could, I thought, look at all this another way. I for one had the impression that a kinship between several fattish people and one thinnish person wasn't moderately unlikely, but extremely unlikely. The expert saw things otherwise, but shared my opinion about the distinguishing features of the ears, which indicated that a parental kinship of the married couple was only a middling possibility. My parents registered marginally negative on the so-called distinguishing features of coloration and integument, which sent Mr Rudolph into a stutter, and which he'd apparently skipped before and not read out at all. My mother didn't want to hear any more details and said it would soon be time for her to do something about dinner. Mr Rudolph said that it was almost over and gave us the news, under the heading 'Contours of head and face', that foundling 2307 bore only a middling resemblance to the woman and a poor resemblance to the man, but a remarkable resemblance to the legitimate son of the married couple. There it was again – what I had feared: Arnold and foundling 2307 respectively were pushing their way into my appearance and hence my life. My fears were reinforced when things reached the area of the chin, which was dissimilar in my father, somewhat similar in my mother, and definitely very similar in me. But to my relief the findings didn't elaborate any further on this. I was beginning to imagine that perhaps I was related both to Arnold and the foundling, but not to my parents. In that case, my mother would not be getting back her lost son, she'd be losing her not-lost son. Then I'd be a sort of foundling too, perhaps even a Russian child. Then my parents would have no more children and I'd have an orphan brother with whom I'd have to share what would probably be some tiny room in a foundling home. But Professor Liebstedt certainly didn't seem particularly interested in my resemblance to the foundling, because he didn't follow up this clue either. What weighed more with him were my parents, and they were the only ones mentioned in the closing summary, which stated that foundling 2307 was 'reasonably unlikely to very unlikely' to be the child of the petitioners. 'That doesn't sound good,' Mr Rudolph said to my mother. She was silent for a moment and then replied with a note of completely unexpected optimism in her voice: 'But not bad either.' Mr Rudolph was a little taken aback and said nothing, and my mother and I said nothing either. Outside it was getting dark already, and soon the searchlight would switch on and light up the cold storage shed. Mr Rudolph looked at the report again and noticed that the

sworn declaration with which the professor had
ended the findings was preceded by one last
observation, which ran, 'This interpolation to the
final statement of the main report does not represent my conclusive expert opinion. This will be
found in a supplementary biomathematical report
to be prepared if required.' Clearly what we had
here was the final report on an inconclusive final
report, which elicited a satisfied 'Just as I thought'
from my mother as she took this in. The very next
day Mr Rudolph put in an official request for
the biomathematical supplementary report. The
report arrived a few days later with another bill.
An accompanying letter from the professor
explained the methodology of the report, which
did not produce evaluations like the main report,
but an 'exact treatment' based on logarithmic
probability rates and supported by a Hollerith
punch card analysis of 130,000 individual items
of evidence. The procedure in this case was to
deal with the married couple separately. The separate treatment specified 'that in one instance the
man will be compared under the assumption that
the mother has a definite consanguinity with the
child and in the other instance the woman will be

compared under the assumption that the man has a definite consanguinity with the child.' My mother read out this passage again, but I wasn't sure if she'd really understood it or only wanted to understand. I had understood it and was surprised that I didn't feature at all in the bio-mathematical supplementary report. Hadn't the professor also had to compare my father and mother with foundling 2307 under the hypothesis that the brother, meaning me, was related to the child too? It's true that I didn't want any definite relationship with the child, but I'd been in Hei-delberg just as much as my parents had, and I'd had my stomach pinched and a screw clamp fastened to my jaw. Now, when we were getting right down to it, I obviously had no role to play any more. Now it was only about my parents and Arnold, who in my view was turning out to be rather self-important. Meantime my mother had passed the report back to Mr Rudolph for him to read out. She seemed to feel overwhelmed by all the numbers and calculations. And perhaps she was also afraid to have to see the report's con-clusion with her own eyes. Mr Rudolph now read out the so-called partial division test values, also

known as PDT values for all groups of distinguishing features. In my father's case it emerged that
out of twelve groups of distinguishing features,
ten tested negative. Only the foot characteristics
and the blood group indicated a relationship with
the 'child', as Professor Liebstedt called foundling
2307, who was still just the 'show-off' to me. My
mother's case was similar, though a little better:
out of twelve groups of distinguishing features,
eight tested negative, while the blood group and
distinguishing features of nose and lips and integument tested possible as to kinship. A further
calculation pulled together blood types and distinguishing features of prints, colour, and bodily
structure in other differing sub-groups and tested
them, as the report put it, 'against statistical bases
calculated specifically for this purpose'. With the
result that the majority of the assembled sub-
groups were negative for both parents, 'the
man', according to Professor Liebstedt, 'testing
particularly poorly according to the distinguishing
features of prints', and 'the woman particularly
poorly according to distinguishing features of
bodily structure'. After Mr Rudolph had read out
this passage, he looked over rather uncertainly at

my mother. But she remained perfectly composed and now asked to hear the rest. The rest was what Professor Liebstedt called his 'final statement', which ran: 'There is a minimum 99.73 per cent certainty, or odds of 370:1, that the petitioners are not the parents of foundling 2307. The husband, taken singly, is also clearly ruled out as the father of this child just as the wife, taken singly, is clearly ruled out as its mother.' This was followed by a sworn statement by the professor and his signature. My mother still remained silent and Mr Rudolph, who was concerned about my mother's state of mind, remarked that the biomathematical supplementary report did nothing but express the finding of the main report in numbers. The findings of the main report, however, stated that a kinship with the child was 'moderately unlikely to very unlikely'. I couldn't see how (though I didn't say so) a probability and improbability respectively of 99.73 per cent had anything to do with a moderate unlikelihood. A 99.73 per cent improbability was something like a total improbability. Now it was no longer undecided, the way it had still been in Heidelberg, it was 370:1 against Arnold. Arnold had scored one goal – the other side 370. If the game was now at an end with its biomathematical supplementary report, then Arnold had flat-out lost, which didn't make me particularly sorry. That my mother had lost, too, certainly made me sad, and I understood that Mr Rudolph wanted to comfort her. But my mother would not allow herself to be comforted. She sat straight-backed at the table, looked at the report that Mr Rudolph had laid in front of her, opened it at the last page, read the results again and, without looking at either Mr Rudolph or me, said, 'I will not allow my child to be taken away from me again.' She didn't say it particularly loudly or with tension in her voice. She said it the way you say something that is self-evident. Now I saw Mr Rudolph, who had stayed rational and calm until now, turn uneasy and start to grope for words. Finally he pointed out to my mother that the proceedings had come to an end with the last set of findings. She had no further legal claim to the preparing of another set of findings and had to consider Arnold as finally lost. It was sad, but that was how it was. She must accept reality. For the first time I heard Mr Rudolph sounding severe. Now he was talking like a policeman and not like someone who spent Sunday afternoons listening to records of operettas with my mother. But it didn't seem to come easy to him. He had to clear his throat and swallow, and sometimes it seemed as if he couldn't get enough air in his lungs as he talked so that he had to stop in mid-word and breathe in deeply. Nevertheless Mr Rudolph's words had made their impression on my mother. She looked first at me, then at Mr Rudolph, then put her hands to her cheeks as if to hold her head steady. Although my mother tried to hold her head with her hands, you could see it begin to tremble again. I had seen my mother's head tremble more than once, but I'd never seen her unable to hold it still with her hands. This time the trembling became so strong that her hands could no longer hold her head and began to tremble along with it. The trembling spread to her arms and shoulders and started to shake my mother's whole upper body, as she tried in vain to still her jerking head with her equally jerking hands. As my mother's trembling intensified I had left my seat and moved away from the table a little. After a first moment of hesitation, Mr Rudolph leapt towards my mother, sat down beside her, and held her so tightly in his arms that her trembling slowly subsided. As he held her, he kept saying, 'It's all right, it's all right,' as if he were talking to a child who'd had a fright. My mother calmed down, and now put her arms around Mr Rudolph and wept quietly. As my mother and Mr Rudolph embraced, I left the room. I would have liked to go roaming through the twisting-and-turning house, but could only run up and down the tiled staircase or go out into the yard behind the cold storage shed where there was the new generator to power the cold storage in case of emergencies. I didn't know what to do while my mother embraced Mr Rudolph. But I was sure that when my mother embraced Mr Rudolph she was thinking of my father. After a time Mr Rudolph left the house too. Before he got into his car, which was almost the same colour as his official car and was also a Volkswagen, he said to me that my mother wasn't feeling well and that we must take special care of her. He wanted to talk to me about everything else in the next few days. But it was almost a week before I saw Mr Rudolph again. He didn't normally let so much time go by without visiting my mother. This time he came in his official car, wearing his uniform. My mother was busy handling orders and settling accounts, and Mr Rudolph used the lunch hour to have the aforementioned conversation with me. At first he said nothing, then he said that I shouldn't be concerned. I didn't know what concerns Mr Rudolph meant. I was concerned about lots of things but Mr Rudolph didn't know about any of them. Then without explanation he put his hands on my shoulders and said he liked my mother and me very much. I felt the blood rise up towards my face, but I didn't want to blush at any cost. Mr Rudolph's words had embarrassed me: there was a policeman sitting in front of me in his green uniform with a service pistol and a radio, saying he liked me. After Mr Rudolph had said this, he seemed to be relieved. He squeezed my shoulders again and then stroked his right hand over the back of my head, which made me worry that he wanted to check out the curve at the base of my skull. But he only touched me for a moment, then took his hand away again and said in a serious voice that the last few weeks had been particularly hard on my mother. She had indeed taken in the results of the report, but he had had to promise her to go on supporting her, which of course he would. Then Mr Rudolph told me that my mother had had the idea of adopting foundling 2307. If the child would not be recognized as her own flesh and blood, then she wanted to adopt it. Deep inside she was still convinced that Arnold and foundling 2307 were the same person. For the 'evident impossibility' of consanguinity referred to in the findings was not the same to her as a proven impossibility. And an improbability of 370:1 and 99.73 per cent respectively was not a 100 per cent improbability. My mother was clinging to the remaining .27 per cent, said Mr Rudolph, and she was clinging to this remaining .27 per cent so tightly that it had transformed itself, so to speak, in the last few days into 99.73 per cent. The longer my mother had thought about the fact that 99.73 per cent wasn't 100 per cent, the more the remaining .27 per cent had become the 99.73 per cent proof that Arnold and the foundling were one and the same. My mother had not allowed herself to be swayed by him and his more clear-eyed view of things and the more he had tried to sway her, the less she had allowed herself to be swayed. Besides which,

the moment he had referred to the conclusions
of the report, she had begun to tremble again, so
that the only thing he could do was back off a
little and talk about the legal situation. But my
mother on the other hand had found it difficult
to accept the legal situation. She had told him
again and again what dreadful things had happened to her, my father, and the child, and that
she did not want to be robbed all over again. The
legal situation was still unfavourable, she had no
illusions about that. Then my mother, according
to Mr Rudolph, had talked about the official
compensation for their sufferings that my father
had filed for after the war and that had been
refused to him because of the legal situation. I
wasn't exactly sure what compensation for their
sufferings was, but I'd heard the expression so
often that it was one of the most familiar of my
childhood. My mother and father had talked
about compensation for their sufferings almost
daily for years until at some point they didn't talk
about it any more. One day the compensation for
their sufferings disappeared from my parents'
lives, but until it disappeared, it gave my parents
no compensation, only real suffering, which

oppressed them and made their lives hard. 'Your mother', said Mr Rudolph, 'hasn't got over the decision about the compensation for their sufferings even today. Not because of the money, because of the justice of it. Justice is all-important to your mother. And now she feels she's been unjustly treated again, although the findings aren't an injustice, they're a bitter fact.' Because he didn't want to risk my mother having a breakdown or perhaps becoming seriously ill, Mr Rudolph said, he'd supported her about the adoption idea. Suddenly he shot to his feet and disappeared, saying, 'Be right back.' Meanwhile I thought about foundling 2307 as an adopted child. I wondered if an adopted child would have the same rights as its natural-born brother. Finally, he was several years older than me and before being plagued by an adopted older brother, I'd rather have been plagued by my own older natural brother. That I'd be plagued by an older brother was for sure. But if it was only an adopted older brother, then maybe the legal situation would be in my favour. I would point out that legally speaking, he was only an adopted older brother. I had decided that already. And if

it turned out that the adopted older brother was
the same person as Arnold, which was still always
theoretically possible, then I would take my real
older brother for a ride and get at him by using
the legal position of an adopted older brother,
which was certainly less favourable than the one
of a real brother. While I was computing the
advantages I had over foundling 2307, Mr
Rudolph came back and explained to me that
because of the adoption question he'd been making inquiries about foundling 2307 these last few
days. The youth service had told him that another
family had filed adoption papers for foundling
2307 years before, but that the adoption papers
had been rejected for as long as the question of
parentage remained unresolved, and for as long as
the legal situation permitted further investigations
of parentage to be commissioned and undertaken.
Things had worked out particularly unfortunately
for foundling 2307, since probable parents had
presented themselves for this child once already
and these parents had also arranged for the relevant expert investigation, which had also turned
out negative. So for all these years foundling 2307
could not be released for adoption and while the

two investigative procedures had come and gone, he was now almost grown-up. Despite all this, the adoptive parents had adopted him anyway. I can imagine, said Mr Rudolph, that the results of my inquiries are extremely depressing for your mother and that she hasn't wanted to talk to me about any of it at all. But he felt it was his duty, and my mother had agreed, that he should explain the whole matter to me, because in the long run I too would be losing a possible brother in foundling 2307. I thanked Mr Rudolph and looked as concerned as I could but underneath I was happy that I had been worrying about the legal situation of adopted older brothers unnecessarily. Nonetheless, the fact that my mother hadn't wanted to talk to me about the adoption question upset me. I was also upset that she still wouldn't make her peace with things. I was here too, after all, and at some point my mother could have said just once that I was here after all. But all I ever heard was that Arnold wasn't here. I was furious at my mother. I was furious at Arnold too. And I realized I was furious at Mr Rudolph too, both because he'd embraced my mother and because my mother had embraced him in a way she'd never embraced me. She'd only squeezed me so tight against her in attacks of despairing mother-love that I couldn't breathe. The foundling had another family now, said Mr Rudolph, and my mother seemed to be slowly taking this in. Nonetheless she had told Mr Rudolph she still had one wish, and he hadn't been able to refuse her. My mother, said Mr Rudolph, wanted to see the foundling just one time. Just one time, she'd said, and he had made her promise that it would be just the one time and no more. 'So where does he live?' I wanted to know from Mr Rudolph but he didn't answer me, and instead explained that in all these years the legal situation had never permitted parents to see the foundling face to face. The relevant youth department had never even told them where the boy lived. But it had been no problem for him to use official channels to unearth foundling 2307's current name and address. 'So where does he live?' I wanted to know again and this time Mr Rudolph told me that foundling 2307 was now called Heinrich, that he lived with his adoptive parents in a little town in the Weserberg land not far from the Porta Westfalica and was finishing his apprenticeship as a butcher in his parents' shop. Arnold the show-off is now called Heinrich and is becoming a butcher, I thought to myself and had to grin. It would have to be Heinrich and it would have to be a butcher. 'What's there to grin about?' Mr Rudolph said suddenly, with a sternness that reminded me of the sternness in my father's voice. I immediately stopped grinning and imagined that Mr Rudolph was slowly turning into my father. In a few days, said Mr Rudolph, in the same friendly voice I was familiar with, he and my mother and I would go on an outing to the Weserberg land. And if everything went well, we could see Arnold or Heinrich or foundling 2307. Naturally from a distance and from the car, unless we went into the butcher's and let ourselves be served by him. I didn't want to let myself be served by Heinrich and I didn't want to see him either. But Mr Rudolph said it would be the best thing for all of us if we went on the outing together. As we got into the Opel Admiral a few days later to drive to the Weserberg land, I had to think back to earlier times. My mother had been to the hairdresser and smelled of cologne, Mr Rudolph was in his civilian clothes, with a hat and a tie, and even I was made to put on my Sunday trousers, although it was Friday. I remembered how often I'd used to get sick on outings, and the facial cramps they'd given me. I tried to recall what it felt like as the first stabs of pain shot into my cheeks and then up into my forehead. And as I thought of the stabs of pain, my face twisted itself into the same evil grin that had always made my father so angry. Before I could even get my face back to normal, I heard the angry voice of Mr Rudolph, who'd seen me in the rear-view mirror. 'Stop that grinning,' he suddenly barked so loudly that my mother got a fright too and turned around towards me. I stopped grinning and knew now that I didn't like Mr Rudolph any more. I didn't pull any more faces and didn't say a word until Mr Rudolph pulled into a gas station to fill up, wash the windshield, and check the oil. My mother and I stayed in the car. My mother was silent, and as I didn't know what to say either, I said, 'Are you going to marry Mr Rudolph?' My mother turned around, her face puffy, looked at me, and said that Mr Rudolph was the person who was closest to her, and that he had been more help to her in the bad times than anybody.

And he had already proposed to her some time ago. She hadn't given him her answer yet, said my mother, but she was going to say no, although she wanted to say yes. Then she turned back to face forward again, and I sensed that she needed someone to comfort her. I was sorry for my mother, but I couldn't comfort her. Arnold should comfort her, I thought, or foundling 2307, or Heinrich the butcher. And before I could even imagine my mother feeling an emotional bond with my lost brother, who had miraculously tripled himself in the meantime, I felt the same guilt and shame again that I always felt when my mother was sad and that made it impossible for me ever to show the smallest sign of closeness to her. Meantime Mr Rudolph had finished filling up and was back behind the wheel again. We drove along the highway that Mr Rudolph always called the Federal Highway and sometimes even the FHW, although I was sure it should be the FH. But I didn't dare correct him. I let Mr Rudolph talk, as he now seemed to be on an even keel again. Clearly filling the tank, cleaning the windshield, and checking the oil suited him. He told us about the Bielefeld–Hannover section of the Federal Highway that we were on at the moment and that ran through the Weserberg area. Mr Rudolph had a colleague who had once served on the Bielefeld–Hannover section of the Federal Highway. And this colleague had often told Mr Rudolph the wildest stories about accidents and speeding incidents, which Mr Rudolph now told me. But the stories didn't interest me. Mr Rudolph's service pistol didn't interest me either. I let Mr Rudolph tell stories about crashed trucks loaded with pigs and milk tankers that ran off the road, but it didn't impress me. Mr Rudolph talked, and I thought about the fact that he didn't yet know my mother would soon say no to him. When we left the highway, Mr Rudolph also stopped telling his stories and concentrated on the local road that took us to Heinrich's new home. The address Mr Rudolph had found said 'the market', so we aimed directly for the centre of town. In the market square, bordered on one side with half-timbered houses but otherwise surrounded by modern commercial buildings and used as a car park, we immediately spotted the butcher's, which was in a flat-roofed building with a glass front. Mr Rudolph parked the car some distance away, so that we couldn't see into the shop. Now he conferred with my mother over what to do. My mother didn't know. I had the sense that what she really wanted to do was drive away without taking a single look into the shop. Mr Rudolph suggested that he go alone and look into the shop first. After a few minutes he came back and said, 'He's in the shop.' My mother said, 'Perhaps it's better if we drive home.' But Mr Rudolph wanted to give my mother her wish. Even if she was beginning to be afraid of her own wish. He turned the car around, left the car park, and drove slowly to the glass-fronted shop, where he stopped. As I caught sight of foundling 2307 through the shop window, I took fright, and realized immediately that Heinrich looked like me. What I saw in the shop was my own mirror image, except a few years older, saying goodbye to a customer. My head spun. I didn't want to believe my own eyes. And I waited for what Mr Rudolph and my mother would say. But Mr Rudolph said nothing. He gazed into the shop with narrowed eyes and a frown and showed no reaction. It was as if he were looking into an empty room. My mother was silent too. Didn't she see what I was seeing? Didn't she recognize her own child again? My head spun. I kept staring into the shop. I felt increasing pressure somewhere near my stomach and smelled the sweetish smell of the artificial fabric from the interior of the car. And as I swallowed and tried to force down my nausea, I saw my double behind the glass go pale as the colour drained from his face. I leaned hard against the back seat, rolled down the window, and took several deep breaths. I wanted to tell my mother, beg her, finally to get out of the car and finally to go in to him. But I had to catch my breath and couldn't say a word. And even as I felt the blood in my head recede and my stomach muscles relax, my mother, who appeared to have noticed nothing, said, 'Close the window. We're leaving.'